The Adver
Benjamin Frank

Author

$\mathbf{M}$arie $\mathbf{S}$killing was born in 1980. She was raised and educated in South West London before studying psychology at Royal Holloway, University of London. Marie always wanted to write, but her studies took her into business and technology. In 2005 she left the UK to live abroad, and her travels gave her the time and freedom to write about her adventures. In 2011 she spent three months in India studying yoga where her writing became less factual and more creative. This shift first appeared in her poetry, but really came alive on a trip to Vancouver, Canada in 2012. It was on this trip that she began her journey with The Adventures of Benjamin Frank.

The Adventures of Benjamin Frank

by

Marie Skilling

From one Ben to another

Enjoy the Journey!

Best Wishes Marie

**Published by
Marmalade Books**

To Mum and Dad,

Thank you for starting the adventure that is my life. It's been a gift of endless opportunities.

I love you both.

Introduction

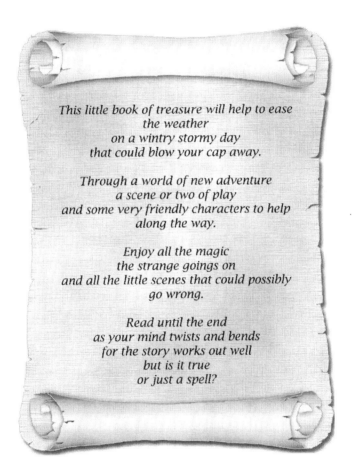

*This little book of treasure will help to ease
the weather
on a wintry stormy day
that could blow your cap away.*

*Through a world of new adventure
a scene or two of play
and some very friendly characters to help
along the way.*

*Enjoy all the magic
the strange goings on
and all the little scenes that could possibly
go wrong.*

*Read until the end
as your mind twists and bends
for the story works out well
but is it true
or just a spell?*

Chapter 1

Frozen to the bone, the cold morning air bites my body as I stand outside my house waiting for the school bus. My face is drenched as the rain pours more heavily the longer I wait. Water streams down the hill towards my feet, seeping into my shoes and making my socks soggy. I hunch my shoulders to shield my neck from the cold and dance from one foot to the other to keep warm.

I hope the bus arrives soon.

My gloves are sodden, making it difficult to peel them back to see the time on my watch. It is ten minutes past and I am going to be late. Why is the bus always late when the weather is bad? I hate being late, especially when it's this cold.

When the bus finally appears through the gloomy cloud I jump up and down with excitement. Its red paint is the only flash of colour to brighten this treacherous morning.

The bus stops right in front of me and I smile as heat pours out of its opening doors. Then Mr John the bus driver shouts his usual, 'Good Morning, Benjamin, isn't this a fine day?' He says it's a fine day whether it is pouring with rain or the sun is shining.

'I don't know about that today, Mr John, but good morning,' I say, as I scramble up the steps to get to my seat behind him.

I live the farthest from school, so I'm always the first to get on and choose my spot.

Mr John is a friendly man, but he doesn't accept nonsense. Nobody has ever tried to make me move out of my seat on his bus, not even the big kids.

The bus windows are steamed up this morning and I can't see the mountains outside. I pull my sports shirt out of my bag and use it to wipe a big circle in the glass next to where I'm sitting.

That's better. I can see now.

I only get to see the mountains on the way to school and I don't want to miss them today of all days. With all the rain down here, I know the snow will fall on the mountaintops and it's one of the best things to watch.

I'd love to play up there amongst the snow, but my parents won't let me. They say I'm too young to go alone, and they won't come with me. But I would have so much fun up there.

I get fidgety just thinking about it.

As I wonder what it might be like to play in the snow, a bright coloured bird appears by my window. Its wings twinkle as they flutter up and down in flight. It flutters close to the bus, and as I watch it I wish I could fly like that. If I could fly high into the sky, way up into the mountains, I'd play in the snow by dipping my beak into it. Then

I'd lick it up as if it were ice cream.

But it's only a dream - people can't fly.

The bus comes to a stop and interrupts my daydream. The doors spring open again and rain sprays in as Spitty Steph steps onto the bus. I can't stand the way she spits when she speaks. I'm not sure why she does it but it's disgusting. I look out of the window to avoid catching her eye. If we make eye contact she might talk to me and I don't want her spit to land on me.

When I look back out of the window the bird has disappeared.

I'd wish my friend Sally travelled with me, as I sometimes get lonely on the way to school. She's in year five as well, but her birthday is before mine. She's already turned ten and goes to a different school but she's my best friend.

If we went to the same school she'd be able to tell me about her weekend adventures on the way. Her father takes her everywhere. They go hiking in the mountains in the summer and ski in the winter.

I asked my parents if I could go with Sally and her father but I'm not allowed.

When the bus stops outside school and the doors fly open I jump off and land in a puddle that saturates my trousers with muddy water. It soaks through and a trickle tickles my legs. I'm sopping wet, but I don't care. I'm too excited to get annoyed today because I'm desperate to get to class as soon as I can.

Miss Timbles is my favourite teacher and

we read adventure books with her. Now that it's the end of term she has promised to show us photographs of her own adventures. She has climbed to the top of the tallest mountains and has abseiled off Table Mountain in Africa.

I can't wait to see her pictures.

When I reach my classroom I'm dripping with rain and mud. The cold water makes me shiver. I check my watch again and have enough time before class starts to run to the toilets and dry myself under the hand dryer.

The toilets are in sprinting distance and I'm there in a jiffy. I swing open the door and speed over to the dryer to slam the big red button to turn it on.

Nothing.

I try it again, but it still doesn't work. We don't have paper towels at my school and I don't want to go into a cubicle and use toilet paper. The only option is to wipe my hands on my sodden trousers. I wipe them up and down my thighs twenty times before my hands are as dry as they're going to get. It will have to do.

When I turn from the dryer to head back to class, I find myself faced with three big kids. They notice my soggy clothes and laugh.

'Ha, did you pee your pants little kid?' asks the largest of the three, his horrible pimpled face staring right into me.

'What a baby!' says his friend who has wide hunched shoulders.

My knees begin to wobble, but I dig deep

within me to find the courage to respond.

'It's raining outside and I landed in a puddle. It's just water,' I say, hoping to get away with it. I dash towards them, my heart pounding as I try to slide past, but the tall kid steps in my way. I look up at his menacing face just as he pushes me backwards to stop me from getting through.

'Where are you going?' asks his other friend. He has spiky black hair and a strange metal ball in his eyebrow.

Before I can answer, an even bigger kid comes crashing through the door and bounces two of the boys out of my way. His thick brown hair covers his eyes so much that he doesn't even notice what he's done. He walks straight over to the mirror as if nothing has happened.

I don't look at him for long, as this is my chance to get away. The tall kid is busy helping his friends off the floor and shouting at the boy who knocked them over.

'Oi, what's your problem?' he shouts, and I don't stick around for the answer.

My legs move slower than normal because the wobbles have started, but I manage to get away.

By the time I get back to class the best seats are taken. In fact, there is only one left. Miss Timbles has set the chairs in a semi circle and I have to squeeze behind the first row to get to my seat. I grimace at Caroline 'Snot Face' Clements who grins at me as I sit down beside her.

Caroline is a nose picker. She picks and

picks all day long, eating every bogy she finds. She's already sliding a loaded finger of snot into her mouth. It's the first time I've had to sit this close to her. I'm close enough to notice a bogie on the back of her hand and I don't want it on my shirt. I lean as far away from her as I can as she lifts the snotty hand to rub her eye.

The bogie ends up in her tangled mousy hair instead of on me and I am relieved. I think about telling her, but if she doesn't mind putting bogies in her mouth, she won't care if it ends up in her hair.

I turn to face the front.

Miss Timbles has started the slide show, but all I can see is the back of Richard 'Frisbee-head' Pritchard. No matter how hard I try, I can't see past his moon head. It is large enough to eclipse the sun anyway, but today of all days, he has gelled his hair into two big spikes. They add an extra inch to his height and make him look like a moonfish or maybe it's a sunfish. I can't remember.

All I know is if I stay where I am, I won't see the photographs.

I try to find another way to see past him, but Caroline is now wiping more snot off her finger onto the underside of her seat. I avoid getting too close to her, but if I move the other way, I'll end up right on top of stinky Basil.

Basil always interrupts class to ask questions that aren't important. But the worst part of all is when he lifts his arm. His armpits smell rotten, like old milk or eggs, and I don't want my nose filled with that.

By balancing myself on the edge of my chair, being careful to keep away from Caroline, I'm almost able to peer over Richard's shoulder. If I can wiggle a little further I'll be able to see. But as I try, Basil raises his hand to ask a question and my nose catches a whiff of his stench. I nearly tumble to the floor.

This is a nightmare. I was so looking forward to this event. If it weren't for the rain and the older boys, I would have made it to class early enough to get the best seat in the front row. But because my morning started out so badly I am now stuck in the worst place possible.

This school drives me cuckoo.

As I slide back onto my chair, avoiding all possible contact with Caroline, I feel defeated. I've waited so long to see these photos, but everything is getting in my way. The only thing I want in the whole world is adventure, but I can't even view photographs of someone else's adventure.

When the slide show is over and class comes to an end, I leave the room, sad about what a failure this has been. Someone hands me an envelope as I walk out the door, but I'm too distracted to pay attention.

All I can think about is the places I'd like to explore.

When my mind returns to the here and now, I look down at the envelope to find my name written on it.

I open it to find an invitation inside:

Dear Benjamin

It's my 10th birthday soon…

Please come along to eat some cake
sing a song and play a game.

From 10-2 we'll have some fun, please
let me know if you can come.

Best Wishes,

Josephine

I turn to face the classroom door and find Josephine stood staring at me through her red glasses, waiting for me to respond. She's new to our class and I don't know her, but I smile and shout, 'thank you,' as I run away.

I'm chuffed! This is my first invite to a party, and if Mum lets me go, it will be my first adventure.

But when I get home and tell Mum about it, I can tell she doesn't want me to go.

But she doesn't say no, which gives me hope and I stare at her, waiting for an answer.

'Is Sally going?' she asks.

'I don't know, Mum. I don't think so. She wouldn't know Sally. The other children are all nice though.'

I made that last part up, as I have no idea who's invited, but I'm desperate to go. It's only a tiny lie.

I wait as Mum thinks about it, but I can tell she still isn't sure.

'I promise I'll do extra homework on Sunday,' I say, which is true because I will do ANYTHING to go.

'Will you now?' she asks, but wanders off without giving me an answer. I follow close behind, hoping she lets me go.

I watch the curls of her long red hair swish from side-to-side with every step she takes. She's so tall it makes my neck ache to look up at her in anticipation of her answer. I rub my neck and nearly bash into her when she stops walking, because I'm following so close.

'Okay, you can go, but you must leave when I'm ready to collect you. No arguments, Benjamin.' Her stern blue eyes stare into mine and I don't disagree. I'm going to have to do as I'm told if I'm to go to this party.

I beam the biggest smile as I run up the stairs two steps at a time. It helps me get there faster, but I can still hear Mum shouting, 'and no misbehaving beforehand or I'll change my mind.'

'No problem, Mum, thanks, Mum,' and I crash my bedroom door behind me with a loud bang.

I am flabbergasted that she's letting me go. This is brilliant. Even Sally will be in shock when I tell her. My first adventure is soon to begin and I cannot wait.

I call Josephine to tell her the news.

Chapter 2

Slamming the car door behind me when Mum
drops me off at Josephine's party, I can hear her
shouting something as I dart off. I don't stop to
listen in case she's changing her mind and doesn't
want me to go.

The party is in a hall near Sally's school.
As I approach the door I can hear music inside the
building. It gets louder when I open the door and
walk into a room filled with people I don't know.

I stand by the doorway for a while, not
knowing what to do. I haven't been to a party
before. Then a tall dark-haired lady walks towards
me.

'Hello, are you Benjamin?'

'Yes, I am.'

'Excellent. Welcome to the party and
please do help yourself to something to eat,' she
says, and points me towards a table filled with
food.

I feel nervous as I walk across the big hall,
not recognising anyone around me. There aren't
any big kids in sight though, which I'm grateful
for, as I could do without their silliness today. The
last thing I need is one of them making life

difficult when I don't know what to do with myself anyway. I need to concentrate on what the others are doing so I know what to do at a party.

When I reach the food table, I search for tasty treats I haven't tried. I'm delighted to find lots of things that Mum doesn't let me eat. There are sausage rolls, crisps, little triangle sandwiches with different fillings, and a big multi-coloured birthday cake with chocolate icing on top.

The first thing I choose has to be something I would regret not having if Mum were to burst in right now and tell me to stop.

I scan the table and find all sorts: balls of cheese, crumbed chicken, scotch eggs and small bowls of wobbly jelly. Then my eyes bulge wide with delight at the site of a messy pyramid of chocolate cupcakes smothered in powder blue icing.

I lunge in to take one from the top, but a piggy looking girl snatches the plate away from me before I can take one. Her eyes are fixed on me as she shovels one after the other into her mouth, not finishing one before she stuffs in another.

I swear she's doing it to tease me.

'Can I have one?' I ask, hoping to get just one cupcake before they all disappear into her greedy little mouth.

'No,' she says, spraying pieces of chocolate sponge in my face. I wipe the crumbs away with the back of my cuff as she pulls the cakes further away from me. Then she stuffs another one into her mouth, and then another until they're all gone.

I end up picking at a sausage roll instead. The rich peppery sausage meat is tasty, but not as tasty as I imagine the cupcakes would have been.

What a horrible girl.

Feeling disappointed I examine the room for other kids from my class, but none of them are here.

Why was I invited? Josephine doesn't know me.

I take another bite from the sausage roll and as I wonder how I ended up here, a bunch of pastry crumbs land on my chin. As I brush them away I continue my scan of the room. I'm delighted when my eyes fall to a familiar face in the corner.

Now I understand how I made the invite list. Sally is sitting in the corner waving back at me with her bright green eyes twinkling away as always.

But there is something different about her today. I'm just not sure what it is.

I pick up a plate and fill it with two sandwiches, a couple of sausage rolls, several scotch eggs, a handful of crisps and two cheese balls. That should be enough to share.

As I wander over to sit on a cushion beside her, I notice she's wearing a light green dress with purple flowers on it. It's one I haven't seen before.

'Hey, Benjamin, I hoped your Mum would let you come to the party,' she says with a big smile on her face.

'Did you tell Josephine to invite me?' I ask.

'Of course I did! She wanted to know if

there was anyone I'd like to invite, so I said you. She lives in a neighbouring street, moved in last month when she joined your school, but she hasn't been happy. The kids in your class have been nasty to her. I told her that you're one of the good ones.'

I notice Sally's hair is all flicky on the ends as it bounces when she speaks. That's what's different.

It suits her.

Before we have time to eat, Josephine announces the start of a game. It's called pass-the-parcel. Her mother instructs us all to sit in a big circle. When we're settled, she hands Josephine a parcel and her father turns on the music.

The parcel is passed around the circle from one person to the next, which seems a funny game, boring really. But then the music stops and a boy with bright orange hair grasps it between his hands. He unwraps a layer of paper and something falls to his lap. He picks it up and holds it in the air. It's a small bag of marbles.

When the music restarts the boy hands the parcel to the girl on his left and then she passes it on to her neighbour. This continues around the circle until the music stops again. Now I understand. The person holding the parcel gets to unwrap a layer of paper when the music stops in the hope of winning a prize. But there are no guarantees because there isn't an item hidden in every layer of paper. A few people unwrap the parcel and find nothing.

When the music stops at the time the parcel

is in my hands, I hope to win something.

I take care as I unwrap it and let out a yelp as something much bigger than marbles lands heavy on my anklebone. Everyone giggles and I'm embarrassed.

But the pain in my ankle and the embarrassment is soon forgotten when I pick up my prize. I have won a wooden kaleidoscope. I put it to my eye and hold it to the light. When I peer through the viewfinder I see thousands of tiny coloured snowflakes in the sky.

It's mesmerising.

When the music plays again, I am too preoccupied with my new toy to notice. I only look up when the boy next to me grabs my attention with a nudge. Everyone is waiting for the parcel to be passed on to the next person.

'Sorry,' I say, as I pass the parcel on to the girl to my left.

When the last layer is unwrapped and the final prize taken, we hand our wrapping paper to Josephine's mother. She tells us all to jump up and Josephine announces the next game.

'This time we're playing Musical Statues, so get ready to do your best dance,' she says.

This is another new game for me, but I am ready for this one because I've been practicing my dance moves in front of the mirror at home. As the music plays I listen hard as I've not heard it before, but I love it. I tap my feet and sway my arms just as I do at home. I really enjoy myself for a while. But then I notice the other kids dancing in different ways and feel uncomfortable. Everything I've practiced disappears from my mind, including how to move my feet. I am frozen to the spot.

When the music stops just like it did when we were playing pass-the-parcel, everyone stands still. I am grateful, as I still hadn't managed to find my dancing feet.

A boy with long arms finds it hard to stay still and Josephine's father announces that he's out. After playing pass the parcel, I understand this game straight away. Good job I'd already stopped otherwise I might have been in the middle of a sway and swayed my way right out of the game.

When the music plays again, I try to copy what the others are doing, but I am off balance and can't match the moves to the music. I worry they'll all laugh at me because I can't get it right. When the music stops I am saved as the tiniest girl in the room wobbles to the floor and she's the next one out.

The pause in the music gives me a chance to think. If I stick to what I know I'm less likely to lose the game. It's a fun game, but I am still anxious. I'll just have to dance the way I know how. Where did they all learn to dance the same way? I suppose they've all been to parties before.

After a couple more pauses in the music, and a further two children leave the game, Sally turns around and dances towards me. Her green eyes twinkle with joy as she copies my moves and we dance in time. Josephine notices us and gives it a go, swaying her long blonde hair in all directions.

The three of us are now dancing together in time to the music. Then the boy with the orange hair joins us.

Before I know it, half the group are copying me and I'm enjoying myself again. It's so much fun dancing in a group.

I manage to hold still every time the music pauses until I'm one of the last two still in the game. But things soon change when Josephine's father stops the music quicker this time to make an announcement.

'Benjamin, I'm afraid you were nearly there, but we have to stop the game.' He points across the room and I turn around to find the unmistakable presence of Mum and her bouncy red curls.

If only she'd come a few minutes later - I might have won the game, but we'll never know now. She could have at least waited until we'd finished. It's so frustrating having strict parents.

Wobbling on my left foot I excuse myself and say my goodbyes as fast as I can. I am so embarrassed to be the only one leaving early.

But what a great party!

Mum waves at Sally when she sees her, and Sally waves back with a friendly smile. When she looks at me her face is filled with sympathy and her hand drops to her side. Maybe if Mum had known Sally would be here she might have let me stay longer.

What a shame. I was so close to winning.

When I climb into Mum's car outside the

hall, and buckle up for the drive home, my excitement from the party has disappeared.

I have now been on my first outing without my parents to somewhere other than school, but I'm not pleased. It was fun, but I only went to another building. I still haven't been on a real adventure.

The snow-capped mountains are visible through the trees as we arrive in silence outside our house.

All I want is to wander up into those mountains and play in the snow. That's a real adventure.

Chapter 3

Bouncing along the road, I have more spring in my step this morning as I head off to catch the school bus. It's Monday, but it's not raining and I'm sure the sun wants to burn through the cloud.

When I notice Josephine standing at my bus stop the day gets even better.

'What are you doing here?' I ask.

'Hey, Benjamin, my mother said I'm allowed to ride the school bus now that she knows you'll be on it every morning.'

If that worked with my mother, I'd be able to explore the great outdoors with Sally and her father.

When the bus arrives I let Josephine sit next to me behind the driver. We talk about lots of different things, including the snow that keeps growing on the mountains.

'It is beautiful, but I don't know if I want to go up that high, and I bet it's freezing,' says Josephine.

'Oh but imagine how it feels. I'd love to wade my way in and leave my footprints in it. Just imagine throwing it all up in the air and watching it sprinkle back towards you.'

'You sound like you'd love to go up there, Benjamin.'

'Oh I would, but I'm not allowed,' and I explain how my parents won't let me.

When we reach the front of school, and climb off the bus, Josephine catches me playing with my mouth.

'What are you doing?' she asks.

'I'm trying to loosen my tooth. It started wobbling in the evening after your party. Mum asked me how many cakes I'd eaten to make that happen, but I promised her I had none.' Which was true even if I didn't want it to be.

'The tooth began to hurt from the minute I woke yesterday morning. I wanted it out of my mouth as soon as possible, so I tried to turn it to make it looser, but it wouldn't budge. It's now stuck at a funny angle.'

I open my mouth wide to show Josephine.

'Oh yes, I see it,' she says, 'but shouldn't all your teeth be out now by now? All my baby teeth fell out yonks ago.'

'It's my last one, and it's taking ages to wobble loose enough to pull it. I keep pushing it with my finger, but all I've done is wedge it in on a twist. Can you see it?' I open my mouth, holding it wide with one finger, and point to it with another.

My eyes are closed, and I don't see the incoming punch heading towards me. It hits me hard in the mouth before I know it and I fall heavily on my side.

My body aches as I lie on the ground. My face is throbbing with pain and my closed eyes don't want to open.

When I eventually force my eyelids apart, my eyes take time to focus. Once everything clears, I spot a bloody tooth on the ground in front of me. I check my swollen mouth and there is a hole where I was trying to push against my milk tooth only minutes ago.

Before I can reach out to pick up the tooth, a large hand reaches down and grabs it from the ground.

The hand belongs to Jungle James. I watch as he rolls the tooth between two fat fingers, the blood wiping clean. He looks delighted behind his Amazonian mop of black, vine-like hair. The whites of his eyes twinkle as much as my now gleaming white tooth that's held out in front of him.

This is the closest I've been to the biggest kid in school. He really does look like the Amazonian people in the books Miss Timbles gives us to read.

When I taste blood in my mouth I sit up and check my clothes for drips, but I'm clear. Feeling dizzy, I try to stand and my legs are surprisingly strong.

Josephine has disappeared, hopefully to find a teacher, though I'm too dizzy to feel scared as I stand facing the mighty Jungle James.

'Why did you punch me?' I ask, nervous that he might do it again.

'I did you a favour dude. You were whining about your tooth not coming out, and now it's here,' he says, holding it high above his head like a trophy. 'You've got nothing but big teeth in your mouth now.'

He's right, but it's my tooth and I want it back. I hold myself tall, straighten out my clothes and surprise myself by coming up with a quick plan.

'I'll do you a deal, James,' I say with a croaky throat. 'If you give me back my tooth, I'll put it under my pillow tonight, and tomorrow morning I'll give you half the money I receive from the tooth fairy.'

'I'd say that sounds like a plan', he says, and places the tooth in my hand.

I turn to walk away.

'Not so fast, little dude, you have to shake on a deal. Hold out your hand with the tooth on it.'

I do as he asks to avoid another punch.

He grabs my hand, turns it on its side and shakes it hard until my body tremors. I worry that my arm might pop from its socket.

When he lets go of my hand, the tooth rolls off and I move fast to catch it before it falls to the ground. I pop it in my pocket to keep it safe. I can't chance losing it before I can get it home and place it under my pillow. Who knows what James might do if I don't have money for him tomorrow. It's not a chance I want to take.

The very next day all is well as I'm able to keep to my word. I give Jungle James one of the two golden coins from the tooth fairy.

'Thanks dude,' he says, and flicks the coin in the air with a smile. 'This is my first ever payment for knocking a tooth out for someone. I've decided it's the start of a brand new business. There are loads of wobbly teeth out there. I reckon a coin per tooth is fair enough. Thanks for the idea.'

As I watch James wander off, I wonder what on earth I've started. I didn't expect him to knock out everyone's teeth. Anyone else with a wobbly tooth will be much younger than me. I only promised him the money so I could get my tooth back.

I suppose the upside is that I'm in the clear because I've lost my last baby tooth. He can't gain anything from the tooth fairy through me.

Even better is that with only one gap to fill in my mouth I'll soon have a full set of adult teeth. It's a sign that I am more than ready to go on an adventure. Plus, if I can make deals with big kids, there's nothing stopping me. Well, maybe Mum and Dad, but Mum let me go to Josephine's party.

I have a good feeling about this.

Chapter 4

Bursting through the front door when I get home from school, I am eager to find Mum and Dad. I must convince them to take me on an adventure. But when I look across the room, my enthusiasm disappears when I find Mum sitting on the sofa in front of the television.

They're not interested in leaving the house with me.

Dad works long hours in the office and wants to relax when he comes home. Mum works from home during the week, so you'd think she'd want to go out, but it's the only time she gets to spend with Dad.

My parents don't even go out to the supermarket. We have our food delivered to the house in bags and boxes. They're not going to take me anywhere and they are not going to let me go alone.

It's so not fair.

Sally sometimes comes over to play with me after school or on the weekend, and her Dad visits my Mum. They're best friends. If Dad was around more often we could go on an adventure together, but he's always too tired to go anywhere.

I spend most of my time at home on the weekend. I love our house that sits high on the hill above the water. The city is just a short ride via a bridge, but I still haven't been. Behind the house is a beautiful thick forest, and the mountaintops are often visible through the trees. There is so much around for me to explore. We live in the perfect place for it.

But at the end of another terrible week at school, I'm just going to go up to my room until I'm tired enough to sleep.

I can see Sally's house from my bedroom window. I look out for her, as I love it when she comes over to play. She's not outside this afternoon as it's still pouring with rain. That's just what it does here in November. I wish I could see Sally's bedroom window, but it's on the other side of the house.

It's been weeks since I saw her.

'What are you doing, Benjamin?' asks Mum as she stands in my bedroom doorway.

'I'm looking for Sally. Why can't she come and play? I don't understand.'

'Don't worry about that,' says Mum with a tone that tells me not to ask again.

'But I want to know what has happened. I'm so tired of being by myself all the time. Sally's my friend and we have done nothing wrong.'

'I know you haven't. It's complicated. Let's leave it at that. You won't be spending time with her for a little while.'

Mum leaves before I can say anything else. I

slide down the wall until I land on my bum and sit wondering about what might have happened the last time I saw Sally.

She was at our house with her father for an unexpected party that Mum organised. It was like Josephine's birthday party, except there wasn't any cake and so I still missed out.

Sally and I played upstairs for most of the time. I was glad because they didn't play fun games like pass-the-parcel. They played music, but when it all got turned off it wasn't because the guests had to stand still until it got turned on again or a parcel was being unwrapped. The music stopped because nearly everyone had already gone home. After that the house just seemed uncomfortable.

When nobody called us to go downstairs, I wondered what had happened.

'Sally, should we find out if it's time for you to go home? I think the party has finished.'

'Why? I'd much rather we keep playing until we have to stop.'

'Something is bugging me; let's peer over the balcony.'

'Okay, Benjamin, but I don't know why you're worried when we could just keep having fun.'

She was right, but I still wandered over to my bedroom door to open it and walk out to the landing. The house was quieter than I expected as we crept to the top of the stairs.

Something was definitely wrong.

We peeped though the twisted wooden banister and listened to our parents talking.

Mum was sitting next to Sally's father on the couch. Dad sat opposite in his big comfy chair.

Everyone else had gone home.

Their quiet chatter was too low for us to hear until Dad shouted then jumped up and left the house. I glanced at Sally who looked as surprised as I felt.

Mum hugged Sally's father then pulled away when Dad flew back through the front door. We had no idea what was going on. Sally's father then called for her to go downstairs. She was with him before I could say goodbye and then it was all over, whatever *it* was. It was strange for our parents to fall out, and I've not seen my father that angry before.

I bet he's the reason why Sally can't play here anymore.

Mum and Dad haven't spoken to each other in front of me since that night, but I can hear them when I go to bed. They fight about Mum being too friendly with Sally's father. None of this makes any sense. Sally's my best friend, but I'm not allowed to play with her and we've done nothing wrong. Why is their falling out our fault? I need Sally to help me plan my adventure.

Even better, I'd love it if she came with me.

Chapter 5

Snow grows thicker on the mountains every day.
I'm desperate to play in it, but nobody will take
me. I haven't seen Sally for ages and I don't know
Josephine well enough to invite her over. I'll go
mad if I don't go out or see someone soon.

I've decided that today is the day for me to
just get on with it and get outside. I don't care if
I'm not the right age or my parents won't take me.

I need to find adventure my own way.

Isn't that what weekends are for?

I look out of my bedroom window for
another glance at Sally's house, but I still can't see
her. My eye catches the mountaintops far beyond
the trees by her house. There's a whole world out
there for me to explore. I could climb trees, chase
animals, and if I reach the top of the mountains I
could dive deep into the snow. I know Sally would
like that. We'd have so much fun.

A little bird appears at my window with the
same bright feathers as the one I saw by the side of
the school bus. It hovers for a moment, staring
right at me, as if waiting for something. It then
shakes its feathers and flutters off again. Flying up
and down then into a spin, it has soon flown far out

of sight.

That bird has the right idea. I'm so tired of being cooped up inside alone. This has been going on for far too long now. My parents can't refuse to take me places, not allow me to go out with other people and not let me see Sally anymore. It's just not fair.

I'm going whether I'm allowed to or not and think of nothing else before sneaking out of my bedroom. I've wasted too much time already.

Once I make it across the landing, I tiptoe towards the balcony and peer through the banister. Mum and Dad are side-by-side on the sofa, snoozing in front of the television. The heat from the open fire is flowing all the way up here. I love the warmth, but if I want an adventure I can't waste this chance. Choosing the right clothes for the weather outside will keep me just as warm. I'll soon forget about the cosy fire.

Treading lightly on the edge of each step, I avoid the creaky middle sections on the stairs. It's a trick I learnt from my trips to Mum's chocolate tin in the middle of the night when I can't sleep and my tummy rumbles. With Mum's expert hearing she can wake at the slightest noise. I creep down the stairs not making a sound.

The tension builds in my chest with every step I take, and my eyes are fixed on Mum, hoping she doesn't wake. I grab hold of the banister leaning most of my weight on it, making me light on each step. It works as I travel down in silence. I am the quietest I have ever been and make it all the way downstairs without her noticing.

My next challenge is to make it across the living room unnoticed. The only way to do this, without making a sound, is to slide along the shiny wooden floor on my bum. It's quite a distance from the stairs to the front door, I wonder if I'll make it unseen? My eye catches a few things I can hide behind along the way, just in case my parents hear me and wake.

I make my first slide across the room and reach Dad's shiny unused golf clubs. The bag is just about big enough for me to hide behind. I peep at the sofa to confirm that I'm in the clear.

This is working well.

The next stage is to reach a tall dresser where Mum keeps her best Christmas crockery. Mum wakes just as I slide behind it. My heart pounds in my chest as I watch her sit up, run her hands through her curls and scan the room for something, but she doesn't notice me.

As I lean on my hands waiting for her to fall asleep again, I touch something under the dresser with my fingers. It's a packet of sweets I lost months ago. I pop them in my pocket in case I need them on my journey.

The last object large enough for me to hide behind is the coat rack. I am filled with excitement when I make it.

I am now next to the front door.

Through the glass pane I can see that the rain has stopped, but it still looks cold. I lift my coat from a hook and button it around me without making a sound.

My boots are shelved low enough for me to reach them, but as I lean towards them I knock the coat rack. I catch it before it falls and pick up my boots. My heart beats faster as my fear of waking my parents increases. I glare right at them with wide fearful eyes, but they're still asleep. That was a lucky escape. I don't hesitate again as I lace up my boots in silence, not daring to breathe.

I can't find my hat and gloves on the rack and I don't want to go out without them. If I look for them I'll only make noise and ruin my chances of getting away.

I spot a floppy flat cap that belongs to Dad. It's too big for me, but it does stay on my head. On the back of the coat rack is a length of green scarf. I grab it and have to wrap it around my neck three times to keep it off the floor. I am swamped in clothing but I won't be cold

A final glance back at my parents confirms they're still snoozing and I reach for the door, just as Dad's gloves catch my eye. They're too big for me, but they'll be warm. After stuffing them into my coat pocket I open the front door to step onto the porch.

The wind is strong outside and it whips the backs of my legs, sending me sailing down the steps. In seconds I am galloping down the garden towards the gate that has blown open.

There is nothing stopping me now.

Out of sight of the house, I run down the hill towards the water, passing lots of cars on the busy road. The wind pushes me on my way, encouraging me to keep going. It's as if it wants me to greet the great outdoors.

I am light and free as I fly down the hill; my face filled with delight for the journey ahead.

Chapter 6

Excited, but cautious, I reach the crossroads at the bottom of the hill and check the road in both directions before I step off the curb. I can see the water on the other side of the park, but not the beach as I stride forwards. I want to run and get there as soon as I can but I cross the road carefully before leaping across the path to land on the edge of the park. It's going to be a sloppy mess getting across the wet grass, but it doesn't matter.

I stomp across the sloshy ground, eager to get to the beach as soon as possible. I avoid a huge muddy puddle in the middle, but my boots are still dirty after a few steps. There are lots of old trees in the park so I stick close to them hoping that the ground near them isn't as wet under the shelter of branches. It helps a bit.

My boots are caked in mud by the time I reach what I think is the beach. It looks like I've pushed my feet into chocolate icing, but I bet it doesn't taste as good.

I ignore the mud, as it won't hurt me, and I start looking for the sandy beach. I'm sure I remember seeing it here when we've passed by in the car. I'm certain it was this side of the park.

Looking along the line where I thought it would be there is nothing but muddy pebbles bunched together with a few scattered logs from the ships in the bay. It's a mess with bits of fishing net, tree bark, and broken glass all mixed up.

It's as if the hands of the sea have rearranged the beach, and they haven't done a good job.

I stand there disturbed not sure what to do
When the tide whooshes in surrounding my boots.

Shaken and stirred I am left in a muddle
As water pours in creating a puddle.

It fills all the space by the glass and the bark
Where the picnics of summer now fade in the dark.

Strangely confused
I am further bemused…

When a shiny crowned penguin jumps from the sea
Landing down heavy in front of me.

I jump back to make way for the first real penguin I've seen. It stands there staring at me with water dripping from its wings. That seems normal. But penguins don't live in these waters. He's a long way from home, which is probably the North Pole.

But more importantly, why is he wearing a lop-sided crown on his head? Penguins don't wear crowns.

I'm sure Miss Timbles would have told us if they did.

'Now now, what do we have here? I don't think you understand who I am,' says the penguin. 'You need to know that I am a p-p-proper penguin of royal magnitude, and I am in for the season to reign on a parade. When I am in town it's important for you to give me a bow.'

'I'm so sorry Sir,' I say, and bow down to this regal penguin.

With my head lowered, I wonder if the penguin is an Emperor Penguin, which would mean he's even further from home as they only live in the South Pole. He is a big penguin.

Then something strikes me on the head and I look up to find a seed bouncing away from me. The penguin has disappeared.

'Where did that penguin go?' I ask, shaking my head and blinking my eyes in disbelief at what I've just seen.

'Oh he's a fickle flipper, fleeting here and fleeting there. He doesn't care. That Little Lord Floppenstein thinks he's the king, but he's merely a kid with a chip on his wing.'

I look back towards the park and the only sign of life I notice is a crow sitting on the third branch of a great oak tree.

'Hey kid,' squawks the crow.

'You can talk? Did you throw that seed at me?'

'Kinda,' he says.

'But why?' I ask.

47

'Well it ain't like I meant to. The bead was in my beak when I bumped into an air pocket and it slipped from my grip. It hit you on its way to the ground. I do apologise.'

'That's okay,' I say.

'Well, I'm sorry about hitting you, but I ain't sorry it scared his *highness* away. He's become a right royal pain in the…'

'Squawk!' screeches another crow as he lands on the same branch and slaps the first one on the back with his right wing.

I look quizzically from one crow to the other, and back again.

'Why are you talking?' I ask.

This is absurd. Birds don't speak, but I've now heard a penguin and a crow talk today.

Before they can answer, a breeze stirs behind me. It lifts the hairs on the back of my neck and brushes them into bristles. They tickle me all the way up my neck to the tip of the top of my head. Before I can smooth it back in place, something tugs at my trouser leg.

Looking down I find a squirrel with a big nut between his sharp pointed teeth. The sneaky little thing climbs up my trouser leg until he reaches my new hedge of hair on the top of my head. I don't like him up there and I tell him, 'get out of my hair, Squirrel!'

But the squirrel isn't listening to a word I say. He is as happy as a squirrel can be, eating a nut, sitting in the softest hedge he has ever known. I dance around from foot to foot whilst flicking my head in every direction, trying to get the squirrel out of my hair.

It doesn't work.

Then out of nowhere a strong gust of wind lifts the cheeky squirrel from my head. It hurts a little as the squirrel tries to cling to my hair, but it doesn't last long and he is soon gone. I expect him to fall hard to the ground, but I am relieved when he is placed gently on the floor. It is so much better to have him out of my hair, but the wind is howling and growing in strength.

As it pushes hard against me, I struggle to stay on my feet.

I hope I don't get blown away.

Chapter 7

Blinking against the force of the wind is the only way I'm able to see, as it grows strong enough to slap me in the face.

I watch as it blows the hairy branches of a magnificent willow tree full force into the air. Its leaves are flying wildly in all directions.

Something about it makes me want to touch it, but I'm frightened I might get lashed by its long limbs.

My intrigue has me taking two cautious steps forward before I stop at the sound of a voice whispering ahead of me. The words appear to be coming from the tree. I can't work out what it's saying, so I step closer and listen hard.

The tree is whispering a message.

'It is windy in the willow -
No more gentle breeze
I sense a something coming
Like waiting on a sneeze.

The hail is yet to bellow
Pouring in a storm
Of lightning proportions - I forewarn.

Don't linger for the showdown
When wicked winds from whirls beyond will crash
in to the land.

It's time for you to go now
For little boys should stay at home
To laugh with joy and play with toys -
Not wallow in the wind.

So hush and mush before the slush
Can knock you flat with boots that squash.

The spell of tides reaches wide -
You must leave now
Run and hide!'

My eyes search for a face in the gloomy strands of the hairy willow tree. But I see neither an ear nor an eye, neither a mouth nor a brow. There is nothing but a splattering of sooty black dust beneath its silver leaves.

'Where will I go?' I say aloud, hoping for an answer.

I search the willowy depths with my windswept eyes to look for a face.

'I've just started my adventure and I don't want to go home. Where should I go from here?' Now I really am crazy - I'm talking to tree! I was talking to birds before that. What is wrong with me?

'Squawk – what should he do, Willow?'

The two crows don't know where I should go either. But I am pleased they can also hear the tree speak even if it means I am hearing birds talk as well.

'Hushhhhhhhhhhhhhh,' whispers Willow. 'This is not a place for little boys - now goooooooo as quick as you can. Trouble will toil with the tiniest first, and you have neither roots to ground you nor wings to free you. How do you suppose you'll stay safe from the whirly wind? It will deliver a tide strong enough to wash you away.'

I stare deep into the willowy shadows where a chunky grey trunk sits deep amongst its leaves. It is layered in heavy bark that looks like chunks of charcoal jutting from its sides. Further up, the trunk turns into branches that loom high above me. They thin until they spill over like a waterfall. Each fine branch is decorated with silver-grey leaves that dance in the wind. They brush my face as I continue forward.

'But where I should go?' I say again, louder this time.

I spot a ledge on the tree where the trunk turns into branches. If I can climb up to it, I'll be out of harms way. I walk close enough to touch the bark and search for a way up. There is a large knot on the trunk I could stand on, but I'm too short to reach it and there is nothing lower.

It's no use.

Then the atmosphere changes, as the air turns heavy, holding me to the ground. The sound of water rumbles behind me and I want to run, but my legs are glued to the mud and I can't get away. Panic sets in and I have no clue what to do.

Then my feet spring free before the incoming water reaches me. My body lifts like a bird even though I don't have wings. It's the willow tree. Its branches are wrapped around me, lifting me high above the ground. It scares me, so I reach out towards the trunk to save myself, but it's too far away. I soar upwards, my legs dangling in the air below me. They begin to wobble, as I fear what might happen.

But when I am placed safely on the ledge, I steady myself and look down to see the tide surging in. It floods the area where I was standing. I am relieved to be out of its way. Sat up here I can dangle my feet with no chance of getting wet, but I'm not comfortable for long.

My body begins to feel giddy and I wobble on the edge. I struggle to steady myself as I'm tipped off balance and something sucks me backwards. It's no smooth ride as my body squeezes through tightly entwined tree branches.

I hope they don't strangle me.

But there is nothing to worry about as the branches ease, giving me space to fit through a great big hole in the trunk.

Inside the tree there are more branches. They fly in all directions and open out to a space much bigger than how the tree appeared on the outside. It's as if the space is limitless with branches flowing in all directions.

I notice tiny golden lights pulsating through them that radiate a wonderful heat. I soon smile as the heat and energy relax me. There is so much life in here. It's like nothing I've experienced before.

Intrigued by the lights, I reach out to touch one of the branches, but it zaps me with a tiny electric shock. It penetrates my fingertips making them throb.

It's a funny feeling that hurts a little, but it also tickles, which makes me giggle.

I'm still laughing when my body is unexpectedly sucked backwards and my breath stops as I charge through a tunnel of flashing lights. I turn and spin as I fly too fast to see. Everything is blurred but lights flash everywhere, making my eyelashes flicker. It makes me uneasy and I feel a bit queasy.

As I am sucked further and further along, I try to reach out and grab something. But as soon as I do, everything disappears and I can't see or feel a thing. The atmosphere calms and I hear a gentle voice singing a song.

'Hush my child and go to sleep
I've saved you now with one great sweep.

Up to Willow you've safely flown -
Free from danger and your woes.

Don't you worry my little charm
In my branches you're safe from harm.

Now close your eyes and rest your mind
Your heart is safe within my bind.'

And with that my eyes close and I drift off to sleep.

Chapter 8

Waking suddenly with a sneeze, I am startled to find myself floating high above the ground. My body jolts like when I've fallen off curbs in my dreams, but there's nothing to fear. Some sort of invisible force is clearly holding me up here.

I can't see it, but it's keeping me safe.

My nose is tickling and I feel the need for another sneeze. I squeeze my nose to stop it and find sooty dust all over my hands. I touch the rest of my face and feel it everywhere.

No wonder I'm sneezing. I clean it off as best I can and look around.

In the distance, far below me, I spot a busy map of tree roots that cross over each other. They're lit with different coloured lights moving in all directions. They appear to be on a journey. When the lights collide they snap and sparkle, bringing the whole tree to life.

It's a fascinating sight.

My eyes dart everywhere, watching the continuous collisions until they tire and I close them to give them a rest.

They don't rest for long though, as they busy themselves by watching the scenes of today flash behind my eyelids. I can see Little Lord Floppenstein, the crows, Willow, and my feet getting stuck in the mud. Then a final gust of wind rolls a huge wave towards me, before Willow's branches lift me from the ground.

Then darkness returns and the scenes disappear.

With my eyes still, my body decides to get busy and begins whirling around in the darkness, like my socks do in the washing machine. All the tipping around sparks a memory of how I got here. I realise for the first time that Willow must have saved me from the whooshing wave before it swept me away.

'I did indeed,' announces Willow.

My eyes open wide at the sound of Willow's voice. There is sooty dust all around me, tickling my nose again. I rub my eyes to help me find Willow, but I can't see him anywhere.

Then I remember I'm inside him. 'Thank you, Willow. That wave surprised me.'

'I know it did, Benjamin. It's a lucky thing I saw it long before it came. That's why I warned you to leave.'

'I know, but because I couldn't see it, I didn't believe it.'

'That's why it's a must you trust. There are many wise warriors who will tell you the why and the how when you need it. You must listen. You're young and will learn lots of things along the way.

Just travel steady and keep your ears open.'

'What do you mean, Willow? Where am I

going?'

'I'm afraid because you ignored my warning, and your chance to save yourself; you're stuck in here for now. Now whistle a tune and be gone with the moon. I'll make sure you're fine, so long as you rhyme.'

'I don't understand, Willow. Why should I rhyme?'

'Your tune will be easier to remember if it rhymes.'

'But I don't have a tune,' I say.

'Ah, but we all have a tune, Benjamin. There's a unique and special one for each of us. Only you can hear your tune. It might drift off key sometimes, but things will come along to help tune you up. Make sure you listen hard and everything will work out well.'

'But how can I listen to my tune if I can't hear it?'

'With time your tune will get louder. It'll be quiet to begin with, but give it a chance and it'll beat strong enough for you to dance. Before you know it, you'll be bopping along to the sound of your song.'

'I like the sound of this, Willow. It sounds like a lot of fun.'

'Oh trust me it is. You'll know what I mean when you get it. Try not to fret about it though, it'll come along at the right time - no point in waiting around for it.'

I am excited about finding my tune and turning it into a song. It sounds like a whole other kind of adventure to go on.

'Let me give you a little taster, Benjamin. Close your eyes and take a deep gentle breath, filling your lungs until they're full. Softly though, I don't want you popping.'

I do as I'm told, filling my lungs as much as I can.

'When you're full to the brim with all the air you need, I want you to release it as slowly as you took it in. Then listen to your sounds.'

I release the air from my chest, taking care not to blast it out too hard. When I'm empty, my eyes open and I smile from ear-to-ear.

'Oh I like the look of that smile,' says Willow, 'but did you hear anything?'

'I did. It was like a beat, but I'd have to do it again to know if it sounds like a song because it didn't last very long.'

'There you go, you're rhyming already. There will be plenty more time for you to find your song. Breathe like that whenever you need to, and before you know it, you'll hear that beat all day long.'

As Willow sings another song, I'm sure it matches the faint beat I can hear inside me.

'Listen now to the beat of your song -
If you sing it and live it you'll never go wrong.

For the wisest of whispers will drum in your ear
a message of reason so quietly clear.

In times of worry or places you fear
the beat of your drum will always be near.

Your senses will lift for your way to be shown
like a voice from above where knowledge is
known.

If you dance with your spirit to the beat of your
song
without a doubt, you will never go wrong.'

I feel every word of Willow's song flow
deep within me. My eyes close and my mouth
smiles. I am ready to move on with my journey.
  'That was lovely, Willow. Now, where do I
go from here?'
  'It is up to you, Benjamin. I'm just an
intervention, a chance encounter that saved you
from the whooshing wave. I can guide your ride,
but I won't dictate your state.
  You now have access to a new realm within
which you are free to explore. You wanted
adventure, now this is your chance. Besides, I am a
willowy old fellow who can only help so far. It's
for you to lead your own way now. This is your
day.'
  'But Willow, I'm still floating in the air.
How am I supposed to go anywhere if I can't
walk?'
  Before Willow answers, I sink towards the
ground until my feet land on a ledge. I am still high
above the roots where the lights collide. It is dark

up here, so I check my surroundings before I walk anywhere.

I don't want to fall off that ledge.

There is nothing around to show me which way I should go. It is dingy in all directions. The light is flat and there are no objects or landmarks in front of me.

'Willow, I could do with some help. Which way should I go?'

Willow still doesn't answer, and for the first time I feel alone. My bottom lip quivers as I realise I don't know where I am. There are no clues to help me either. I think as hard as I can about what I should do. When I said I wanted adventure I thought about trees and snow, not darkness and soot. Then I remember Willow's lesson.

I take a deep but gentle breath in.

Chapter 9

Filling my lungs with air brings a whole pile of thoughts to my brain. I think about how odd it is to be inside a tree. But then there's nothing normal about my recent experiences. I've spoken to a tree and several birds.

It's all rather odd.

I think back to my plan before I met the birds, but I don't suppose I had one. I just had a desire to find adventure. To where, well I hadn't got that far. The idea was about exploring as I went along. I didn't have to know where I might end up. That is the adventure. But now I'm out here, with nothing stopping me, I don't know where to start.

This is harder than I thought.

I laugh out loud as I think about all the crazy events I've experienced today. They certainly weren't part of any plan.

'A penny for them!' says a voice from the darkness that silences my laughter.

'A penny?' I ask. What could the penny be for? It can't be for another tooth, as I don't have baby teeth left in my mouth. Not that I would accept a mere penny for a whole tooth anyway.

'A penny for your thoughts,' continues the

voice.

I'm worried about how many people (or animals and trees) can read my thoughts.

'Who are you, and why are you reading my thoughts?' I ask.

'I am a figment of your imagination, and that is how I know what you're thinking. I'd like to buy some of those thoughts you're having. They seem like interesting adventures you've been on.'

'That's impossible. How can you know what I'm thinking?' I ask, though I can't see who I'm talking to.

'Your brain created me. I'm part of your imagination, which makes you my master-maker.

I'm here because of you and I'm part of you.'

'What on earth does that mean?'

'It means I am what I am to you because you have created me that way and I'm here because you'd like me to be.'

'Is that right?' The voice is familiar, but I can't quite place it. I search for a person to match the voice, but I can't see anyone. I try to screw up my face to see better, but it doesn't work.

'Stretch your mind instead, Benjamin.'

'How do I stretch my mind? I might not have enough space in my head for that.'

'It's a metaphor, but let me put it another way. Do you dream?'

'Yes, I dream. Everyone does'

'Absolutely! So, as you do in your dreams, let your mind wander to all the places of possibility. Think beyond the familiar. Isn't that what you've been waiting for? You wanted an adventure outside of your home, to wander into the unknown. Why don't you do that?'

The voice is right. I've longed for something different from all I've known so far. I flick through all my thoughts of where I've wanted to go. Miss Timbles made Africa look amazing. Jungle James has always made me curious about the Amazon. Brazil would be a great place to visit. The snow makes me want to learn how to ski.

But none of that matters right now. Who is this person talking to me?

I search my memory for where I've heard the voice before and a picture soon burns bright and clear. Then a creature of my imagination begins to emerge in front of me.

I can't quite see the face, but the body is very much a bird, though this one has arms as well as wings.

'Well done, Benjamin,' says the voice.

The voice now sounds more familiar than before, but its face isn't clear. As the face develops it looks different to the bird I saw before.

'Sally!' I shout, taking care not to fall off the ledge with all the excitement.

'Hello, Benjamin.'

'What are you doing here, Sally? I've missed you so much.'

'Well, I came to your house, as I do every day but when I arrived you were whirling away.

I followed close, as close I could
but you flew so free as I hoped you would.

I followed you down to the pebbled beach
but the tide had rinsed all the sand in its reach.

Then I fell on my bum when a penguin appeared
so I hid by a tree for he frightened me.

And that was nothing compared to the wave
the wind with its billow
and the whispers of Willow.

So I leapt from the tree as fast as I could
and grabbed on your bootlace as only I would.

Of course I fell in a whirly-swirl
but here I am now: your favourite girl!'

'What do you mean when you say you
come to my house every day?' I am flustered by
this new information, and I'm blushing. Sally
knows she's my favourite girl.

'I often come by your house hoping to
bump into you. The falling out between our parents
has nothing to do with us. You're still my best
friend.'

'And you are mine, but I haven't seen you.
I've searched the street for you from my bedroom
window so many times. I don't know what
happened either, but it doesn't matter now, let's
find something to do.'

'I can't stay. I left home hours ago and my

father will worry. He'll wonder where I am.'

I can't believe Sally is leaving me so soon. 'You're always welcome at my house in my mind, but I have no say over my parents. I'm just glad you're here now, but if you're going home, why don't I come with you?'

'You can't leave yet, Benjamin. I think there's more for you to see here.'

With that, a whirl of glitter spins into a dusty swirl above Sally's head and she disappears into it. I had hoped she would keep me company on the journey, but she's gone.

Maybe she's right; perhaps I have to go on this adventure by myself. After all, being alone doesn't mean being lonely.

Exploring the world is more important to me than anything, and this is as good a place as any to make a start. I take a deep breath and choose the sensible option of walking forwards, making sure I stay well away from any edges.

A signpost to guide me on which way to go would be nice, but it's too dark to read one anyway. Besides, I've not been here before and I wouldn't know the place names. Skipping towards the darkness, I am soon on my way to somewhere.

With each step I lift my feet high above potential obstacles. My body is a little quivery, as I shiver on forwards, but I decide that there will be no wobbling today.

The last thing I need is an unexpected punch from Jungle James.

Chapter 10

Travelling along for what feels like forever, I'm still not sure where I'm headed. When my feet begin to land in wet splotches that splatter up my trousers, I find it strange. It hasn't rained since I left home or entered Willow. They can't be puddles. My boots squelch with every slippery step, just like they did when I crossed the muddy park, but the ground is too hard for grass and mud.

The next thought that springs to mind doesn't put a smile on my face. What if they're puddles made from Spitty Stella's spittle? It wouldn't surprise me if she were around, spitting lots of puddles all over the ground.

The wet blobs grow larger the further I travel. They grow so big that I have to take two or three steps through each one. Then I step into another that is bigger again. They're far too big to be spit puddles.

I soon notice a change in the texture under my feet and I can hear a crunch with every step. It's as if something is sticking to the bottom of my boots. I try hard to work out what it is as I continue to walk. With every step I take the sky seems to lighten.

I hope I'll be able to see better soon.

When I feel a gentle dusting across my face, I touch my cheeks to find out what it is. It is dry and powdery, but turns wet in an instant. What could it be?

As the sky brightens further, I'm able to study it.

More of it falls from the sky towards my face and brushes my cheeks before drifting to the floor. I smile because I now know I am looking at snow.

My eyelashes catch little pieces before I blink them away to help me see every beautiful flake that falls towards my face.

It's a pleasure to see such a magical thing.

I stretch out my hand to catch a snowflake and inspect its details. The first one I find is too small, but the next one is large enough for me to observe.

Its maize of connecting lines forms a pattern from the centre to the edges. I catch another one, which differs from the last. Then I reach out for another, and it is different again.

Every time I catch one it is so different from the ones before. I want to save them and take them home to put in a collection, but they all melt soon after landing in my hand.

I'll just have to enjoy them for as long as they last.

In the time it takes me to inspect the snowflakes, many more have fallen to the ground.

A deep layer of snow has formed around me. I step into it to find out what it feels like. I've waited so long to see this, and now it's in front of me I can find out for myself.

My feet and legs make channels through the snow as I wade in. It is light and fluffy and moves out of my way with ease. I want to make footprints in it, so I lift my legs high above the snow level to print my feet back down. I keep going until I find myself in the middle of a garden with a trail of footsteps behind me.

I've wanted to do that for such a long time.

After being in the dark for so long, my eyes take time to adjust to the light reflecting off the snow. When they do, I am in awe of this beautiful scene. The snow is whipped into a blanket of creamy egg whites on the surrounding ground. There is a house at the far end of the garden, similar to the ones on my road, but there are no footsteps leading to it. It looks empty.

The snow is more beautiful and fluffy than I imagined it could be. There are huge pillows of it and I want to dive into them.

I am so lucky to be here and watch it glisten in the light.

'Don't you want to play in it?' asks another familiar voice.

'Josephine? Where are you? Sally was here, but you've missed her. She went home.'

Looking around the garden I can't find Josephine anywhere. I call out to her again, but she doesn't appear, so I drag my feet a little further through the snow, hoping to find her. Josephine appears through the trees with the most beautiful snowy owl on her shoulder. Its head spins around to look at me, revealing its huge round eyes that blink wide and bright. I stare back. Something about it draws me towards it.

As I wade through the thick snow I am determined to touch it.

When I get close enough, I reach out to stroke its wings. But when my fingertips touch its beautiful feathers, its wings begin to flap. They hit my body, making me fall backwards. I land on what feels like a pile of soft owl feathers. But a big puff of light powdery snow whisps around me and I know I've landed on a snow pillow.

With every flap of its wings the owl appears to be growing. It grows so big that I can no longer see Josephine who is hidden behind its wings. I watch in wonderment as the owl lifts higher, up into the sky. Its wings grow so large that they bash together and the owl turns into a large ball of snow that explodes in the air.

Millions of huge snowflakes sprinkle their way towards me and twinkle across my face. It is such a lovely feeling, but it's a shame Josephine had to go.

As the snowflakes fall they turn into familiar objects that float around me. There are dishes and cups to my left, knives and forks to my right, and an umbrella flying overhead. A sock floats out of a boot, just as a string of pearls wrap around a poodle's neck. When a large chair lands next to me, I grab it to pull myself up, but it crumbles to the ground. Then a herd of the tiniest ponies gallop over my shoulder.

In the distance, I spot furniture and cars of all shapes and sizes. Then a bat hits a ball towards me. The ball hits me on the shoulder before I can move, exploding like a snowball into a snowy dust. The dust reforms into a new object. It's a paintbrush. The brush springs to life and paints new items in the sky: hats, scarves, gloves, shoes, a flower, sunglasses and then something that looks like my mother's hand mirror.

I jump up to grab its handle before it disappears.

Although the mirror is made of snow, it somehow reflects my face back at me.

I look into it to study my features like Mum does with hers every day. My eyes are as blue as hers and I have hair as dark as my Dad's. When the sun lightens it, I sometimes notice a bit of red in my hair, like Mum's, but not today.

'What are you searching for, Benjamin?' asks a voice from above that sounds like Sally.

'I don't know,' I say, looking up, but I can't see anyone.

'Then why do you stare into the mirror?'

'Well, my mother stares at hers so often that I assumed it gave her many answers. I saw this mirror and thought I might find answers myself.'

'What are your questions?'

'I don't have questions,' I say.

'Search a little deeper into the mirror; what

do you see beyond your face?'

When I look into the mirror I expect to see reflections of the things behind me, but they're not there. Instead, the closer I look, the deeper I travel until I am transported from the snow towards a wonderful green path in a forest. It feels like a dream. I jog along the path until I reach the snow again and fall into it. I fall backwards until I drop out of the mirror and land on a soft cushion of snow back in the garden.

I drop the mirror and it shatters into teeny-tiny pieces on the ground.

'Oh no! I will have seven years of bad luck,' I shout.

'Nonsense!' says the voice.

'But that's what Mum says will happen if I get under her feet when she's looking into her mirror.'

'Oh that is just an irksome old tale - certain to scare you, but one to ignore. A mirror breaks when a person stares into it for too long or looks in vain. Mirrors reveal more in you than you will ever see in them.'

'But mirrors don't have eyes,' I say.

'That is true, but if we try hard enough, we can see far more than just what our eyes can show us.'

'Really?' I ask.

'Yes. We can perceive the world in more ways than one. A mirror has perfected the art of revealing things to our eyes, but it can reflect so much more. The things you saw, what did they tell you?'

I can't be talking to Sally; she's clever, but this is real grown up stuff. But then her father might have taught her lots of new things on their adventures.

'Adventure! That's what I saw. The mirror showed me a journey. There was a path through a forest that led me to more snow. I've wanted to go on an adventure for such a long time. It was showing me what's in my heart.'

'Well that sounds like magic,' says the voice.

'Magic?' I wasn't so sure. It seemed more like one of my school bus daydreams.

'The other thing to remember, Benjamin is that everything is temporary: a bad day, a good day, they're both just a day. When they end, a new day begins. When that new day begins we get to start over again. Isn't that great?'

And with that the shattered pieces of glass join to form a whole new piece. Then a frame grows around it and a brand new mirror is formed. The frame then sprouts a pair of wings before taking to the skies to meet the other floating objects.

'Interesting, isn't it?' says the voice.

'Yes,' I say, remembering I still haven't worked out if I'm talking to Sally or someone else. I look around again, scanning the sky for the voice above me, but I can't see anything or anyone.

'There's one last place to search, Benjamin.'

This time I know where the voice is coming from, and I think I'm quick enough to catch it.

With one wild swing of my arms, up into the air above me, I slap my hands together, catching something between my palms. But I release it because it wriggles and is making my palms tickle until I want to scratch the tickle away.

'That was a nasty thing to do!' shouts the voice.

Oh dear, I'm in trouble now. Sally's face is close enough to mine for our noses to touch. She has appeared again as the tiny little creature I saw before, flapping her wings at such a speed they are almost invisible. Her arms are crossed, and a very unhappy scowl is spreading across her face.

Despite her beautiful peacock green and deep purple feathers, she appears red with rage.

'I should feed you to the Esquimalts, Benjamin Frank!'

'The what?' I ask.

'The Esquimalts! Are your ears blocked?' Sally doesn't seem impressed with me and I've not heard her speak like this before.

'I heard you all right, Sally, but I don't understand what you're talking about.'

'Well, you'll soon find out if you keep up with that kind of nonsense!' She is really shouting now.

'What do you expect if you flutter out of sight? Tell me what an Esquimalt is and I'll forgive you for starting all of this.'

'Forgive me? You squashed me!' Her eyes

are popping out of her angry little head and I don't know how to calm her.

'Esquimalts are nasty little creatures that live along the shoreline. Every time the water shoals over the rocks, their razor sharp teeth gnash at the air and bite all in their reach.'

'Ouch! Why would you want to feed me to something like that?' I am hurt that my best friend would do that.

'You tried to swat me like a fly. What do you expect?'

'I didn't know I was going to hurt you, Sally.'

'Hmmmmmmmmmm.'

'It's true. I heard your voice and thought it was you at first, but I couldn't see you. When did you learn to fly?'

'I've always had wings, and you've seen them before.'

'Have I? When? Do you mean earlier? I thought I was dreaming then. Anyway, why do you have wings and feathers?'

'What do you think I am? What do I look like?'

'A bird?'

'Are you asking, Benjamin? What do you see in front of you?'

'A bird!' I shout.

'Yes, I'm a bird. I'm a fairy bird to be exact.'

'A fairy bird - what is one of those? This is weird. You're not a bird. I'm imagining this.'

Sally doesn't share my confusion for the weirder than weird things going on and sings me a little song to tell me so.

'You know…

I could humph and complain
For this isn't a game
But I'm light and airy with wings like a fairy.

I'm a bird with flight reaching great heights
So I hum and I sing for the joy that it brings.

For flight is free
As are we
So follow your nose and smell a rose.

For to stop and look you will certainly see
That there's nothing to stop you from living your dreams.

Drop all your rules -
Your imposed restraints
Kick off your boots and dance in the rain.

For life is too short to weep in the willow
Live with the breeze and its changing billow.

For surprises occur at the drop of a hat
You just need to listen -
Now fancy that!'

I follow her every move as she flutters and flaps, spins and soars to the words of her song. I smile as I watch her. She has the breeze under her wings, and I am in awe of her as she flies so freely.

Then I remember where I've seen her before today.

'The bird!'

'Didn't we establish that?' she asks.

'No, that's not what I mean. I saw a bird. I have seen you before, and you looked like a bird. At least I think I have. Are you the bird I saw from the window of my school bus? Your feathers look the same.'

'Perhaps,' she says, as a broad smile spreads across her cute little face.

'You were there again when I looked over to your house, hoping that you'd come over to play with me. It's as if you were coming to see me every time I missed you. I didn't realise it was you because you were a bird, and well, I know you as a girl.'

'You might be right, Benjamin.'

'Wow! To think I was missing you, but you were with me all that time. It doesn't matter that you're a fairy bird with wings and feathers. You are my friend, and a dear one at that.'

Sally is blushing and looks awkward in her pretty feathers.

'Thanks, Ben,' she says, as she peers out from beneath her purple eyelashes.

'Can you stay here with me, Sally? Please don't leave again. I'm sorry I nearly squashed you.'

'I can stay with you until there is no need

for me to be here. You'll be fine without me. You are as free as I am, Benjamin.'

'How am I as free as you?' I don't feel as free as Sally appears to be. She has grown wings and I'm still standing here like a boring old Benjamin.

'You don't need to turn into something else to be special. You are special - believe it.'

She's right; I can do this alone. But I also know that a journey shared with Sally would mean so much more, even if she does now flutter instead of walk.

Chapter 11

Fascinated to have Sally fluttering by my side instead of walking, I pay little attention to where we're going until she directs me towards a dirt track.

I slip with the first step, as there are lots of tiny stones that roll under my feet. Giggling, I lose my footing but manage not to fall. It's trickier than walking through snow.

Sally beats her wings to get ahead of me to check which way we should go next. She turns left towards the trees and I follow her, happy in my self and curious about where we're going.

'Where are you taking us?' I ask.

'We're entering the Chillywhack Forest. It's an easy path, but keep your eye out for the odd branch. They sometimes lay across the path and you don't want to trip.'

As the path winds downwards, I hop and jump over a few obstacles. I find more than just the odd branch. I bounce over stones, leap over trickles of water, and jump across logs buried amongst the wet brown leaves that cover the ground.

This trip is so much fun. It's exactly what I've been hoping for: an adventure into the great

.outdoors.

'I love it in here, Sally. Can we stay for a while? We could build a tree house and sleep overnight.'

'We will be in here for a while, but I'm afraid we can't stay overnight. It's important that we keep moving. It's that time of year when it can go one of two ways. We'll either be hit by a cold snap or it'll warm up and the bears will wake. You never know which way it could turn and either way, we need to stay safe.'

'Bears?' I ask.

'Yes.'

'I want to see one. Can we look for one?'

I am wild with excitement at being able to find a real bear.

'It's chilly today. I'd say they're still hibernating underground. We would need to stop and wake one to see it, and it's getting colder around here. I'm worried about a cold snap surprising us. We should keep moving.'

'Oh, Sally, please can we try? Just for a minute or two.' I grin with all my teeth showing in an attempt to persuade her.

'Oh okay, but we must be quick. You can listen to one rumble under the ground. The bears are grumpy and grizzly around here and I'd rather be gone before one of them gets out of bed.'

I smile and nod in agreement as Sally flutters off to inspect a large rock. She hovers above it then dips down behind.

When Sally reappears, she nods and says, 'come and stand on this rock.'

I sprint over, thrilled by the prospect of seeing a bear.

'Now stamp your feet as hard as you can.'

I do exactly as I'm told until she spreads her wings wide and puts her hands up, her rosy little palms suggesting I should stop.

'Now wait and listen,' she says, as she rubs her hands in anticipation. Her wings are beating fast.

'I can't hear anything,' I say.

'Give it another go,' she says.

I stamp my feet harder this time. I so want to see a bear and this might be my only chance. I pound my feet at a rapid rate and stop when the ground rumbles beneath me. Sally watches my face with wide eyes.

'There you go. That's the bear banging back. You've just woken your first bear, Benjamin.'

'That's a big rumble for someone half asleep. Is this a good idea?'

'You were the one that wanted to wake a bear. Don't worry, it's far too chilly for one to leave its den and appear above the ground. We won't come to any harm.'

But Sally is wrong.

'Sally, I think maybe this bear was just resting.'

As the head of a bear appears from a gap between two rocks, Sally is unaware of it rising behind her.

'Yes silly, bears do that when they're hibernating.'

'Sure, Sally, but there's a difference between a hibernating bear, and one that is just taking a rest.'

The bear is growing in size behind her, but she still hasn't noticed. I'm not sure how to tell her what's happening for her to believe me.

Then I remember what Willow taught me and take a calm breath as I try to listen to what the beat of my tune is telling me. I decide to get straight to the point.

'Think what you like Sally, but the bear is right behind you, and it looks grizzly. I'm leaving right this second.'

And with that, I run as fast as I can, whilst Sally flicks to face the bear head on.

'Oh, Benjamin! Run. Run as fast you can.'

I'm already running as fast as I can, leaving Sally way behind me.

'Fly, Sally, fly!'

Sally can fly high above the bear, and escape its reach, but he could catch me. Sally knows it too and plans my escape.

'If I flutter and flap I'll bring the bear to my trap
Where I'll lure him in close to ensure he's engrossed.

And in that time, Benjamin will flee
For the bear will focus completely on me.

When Benny is free I will make my way -
Through the skies above
Just like a dove.

Then I'll find dear Benjamin down by the sea
Sitting in peace by the trunk of a tree.'

I hope she's right and her plan works. I run towards a big tree to peer out from a place of safety. Sally is fluttering her wings hard, and the bear is fixated on her. I am lucky, as he doesn't seem to have noticed me.

Sally flaps around his head making the bear more and more confused. I worry as his huge paw lifts into the air towards her. He could swipe her from the sky with his paw that is big enough to cover his face.

As it lifts, I worry for Sally's safety. His mouth is now opening wide. But it's okay; he's just yawning and is polite enough to cover his mouth. It is the loudest yawn I have ever heard and my ears are suffering all the way back here.

Now that the bear's eyes are closed, I use the opportunity to make a run for it. There's no need to hang around to find out what happens when the yawn is over and he can see us again. I run as fast as I can, not fearing for Sally. She'll flap her little wings hard and fast to keep out of harm's way.

She'll soon catch up with me.

As I run faster than I ever have before, I hop and skip over everything I see by my feet. To fall over now would be disastrous, as the bear could grab me.

I pick up my pace and surprise myself by how quickly I can run.

Chapter 12

Popping free of the forest, I land on a large boulder out in the open. Hundreds if not thousands of smooth red boulders that stretch along the coastline surround me. Climbing from one to the next, I discover a pool between two of them. The water reflects the perfect blue sky and the details of my face. I lean in to investigate the things under the surface.

I am thrilled to find several electric blue starfish. Their blue is brighter than the sky and they're covered in little bumps with a tiny orange spot on the top of each one. They're amazing. I daren't touch them in case they're poisonous, but I study their texture and wonder how they go about their adventures. But when they don't move for quite some time, I begin to think that maybe they don't go very far.

I jump across to another rock closer to the bay in search of new creatures.

I find seaweed, lots of shells that are stuck to the rocks and some funny little red squishy lumps that suck my finger when I touch them. This is what I call an adventure: finding unexpected animals and experimenting with whatever I find.

I love learning new things outside.

As I step along, I breathe in the fresh air, and before I know it, I have landed on a large flat rock where I find a lone tree by the edge of the sea. I am tired after running and jumping from one rock to another and decide to lean against the tree for a snooze in the sun. I sit down and rest my head against its trunk.

It's sweltering hot.

As I move to undo my coat, pieces of bark flake over me. I brush some of it away, but my eyelids lower before I can finish. My body relaxes, exhausted by the heat of the sun, and I am soon fast asleep.

Sally's voice is the next thing I'm aware of.

'Well I'm very grateful that you trusted me to distract that bear. But had I not been able to, a snooze of this nature would have been unsafe, Benjamin. The bear would have eaten you for supper.'

I answer her without opening my eyes.

'I trusted you, Sally. If you can turn into a fairy bird, complete with feathers, wings and hands, I was certain you could distract a bear. Besides, I'm also where you said I would be in your song, 'sat under a tree, snoozing in the sun, down by the sea.'

I open my eyes and smile, waiting to see what impact my words have on her.

'That is true,' agrees Sally, as she nods with delight at her accomplishments. Her feathered wings beat fast with pride, as she sparkles in the sunlight with all her colours dazzling bright.

I look around as I soak up the sunshine. We have found such a beautiful place. There are ships in the bay, and the sun is twinkling on the water. It is cloudy in the distance, but even that looks pretty as it moves low towards the water. The tops of the city skyscrapers are poking through what looks like a blanket of cotton wool wrapped around the buildings.

It's a fascinating sight, and as my eyes scan our surroundings it soon becomes clear where we are.

'We're almost home, Sally.'

'What makes you think that?' she asks.

'Look,' and I point my finger towards the water.

'From where I'm sitting, I can see we've travelled to the forest at the end of the path that follows the water. Based on where we are, and where the city is, I'm guessing we're between the two. In fact, I can almost see my house over there.'

But as I point it out to Sally, the cloud moves and it is hidden once again.

'I think you're right, Benjamin, but there is one problem with this picture.'

'What's that?' I ask.

'Where we live is now buried in cloud. We can't go back the way we came, and we'll never find our way home if we head into that fog.'

'Why don't we get a boat?' I ask. 'With all these ships in the bay, there must be a small boat available to take us home?'

'Not from here, I'm afraid. Boats can't pull up to these rocks without getting smashed. But I know where we can catch a water taxi to take us home.'

'A what?' I ask.

'A water taxi; it's a tiny little boat with a flat bottom. They're light enough to sit on top of the water and zip people around from one place to another. We'll be able to find one on the river and be home in no time.'

'What river? Anyway, don't we have to go back towards the city? I didn't notice a river in the forest. I'm sure we can head back the way we came and make our way back through the fog.'

'The only way is via the river. We'd disappear forever into that fog that will only grow thicker. Besides, the river isn't far from here. We need to go back through the Chillywhack forest, but in the opposite direction. Water taxis are always on standby over there.'

'Great, let's go,' I say.

'Okay, but be warned, it's not the easiest path to follow, and it is called the Chillywhack Forest for good reason.'

'And what might that be?' I ask, wondering if I actually want to know.

'Because the cold snaps I mentioned can come in faster than you're ready for, and whack you harder than you can stand.'

'But it wasn't cold in there a minute ago,' I say.

'Like I said, it's when you least expect it. Fasten your coat, pull on your gloves and tighten your scarf. We have no choice but to go through.'

'What about the bear?'

'I'd like to think we've already had that experience today and our chances are more in favour of a cold snap.'

Sally always makes good sense of these things. I nod, tighten my scarf, pull on my gloves, and zip up my coat.

'Right, let's go - I'm ready!'

Sally flips her fluttering body around and leads me back towards the forest. But as we turn, she stops stiff in the air, pausing as she looks up then retreats back to me.

She perches on my shoulder, shivering like a leaf about to fall from a tree.

'What's wrong?' I ask.

Sally moves as close to my ear as she can, and hugs the side of my face with her little arms, her wings tucked close to her body. She has made herself so small I can't see her.

Taking a deep breath that tickles my ear, she whispers, 'don't make it obvious, but look up. What can you see at the top of the trees? I can sense them, but if I look they'll become real, and I don't want them to be real.'

I look up and shout with excitement, 'wow there are two bald eagles sitting side-by-side. That's amazing! I've always wanted to see a bald eagle. This is becoming a great adventure.'

'Shhhh, Benjamin, stop shouting. In this

outfit I am dinner to them. Now tiptoe so they can't hear you. I don't need their attention on me, okay.'

'Why don't you change your outfit? You've already changed from a girl to a bird. How about a wolf? The eagles would soon hide from you if you were a wolf.'

'Hey land animal, I like my feathers just the way they are. It's your turn to keep me safe now.'

She's right. She's the perfect size for an eagle's lunch, but small enough to hide in my coat pocket where I can keep her safe. I pluck her from my shoulder, knowing she probably wants me to stop but is too fearful of alerting the eagles of her presence, and I place her inside.

Casting my gaze back up to the eagles I am in awe of their freedom. My eyes are fixated as one of them spreads its wings to let the other one preen its feathers. The sun glows on them creating a magnificent sight.

'Beautiful,' I say aloud without realising, as I stare at them, my feet no longer walking.

'Please keep your eyes on the road and your feet moving, Benjamin,' whispers Sally from inside my pocket. 'I can't afford to risk you falling over and making a spectacle of us. If I fall out of your pocket, they'll take one look at my feathers and eat me on the spot. Now let's get out of here.'

'Okay, Sally. Sorry. I understand now.'

'Finally,' she says, and I know her well enough to sense she is rolling her eyes at me.

Chapter 13

Warming up as we walk through the forest, I want to remove my coat and scarf as beads of sweat build on my forehead. But I stop when I realise how difficult it would be to run from a bear if I'm carrying my clothes. My ears twitch at the thought of it and I listen out for rumbles underground.

The beat in my chest grows louder and stronger than anything I have ever felt before. I take deep gentle breaths to calm myself. What a great trick Willow taught me for these tricky situations.

When the beating slows, I don't feel as scared, which I think means I've learnt how to listen to my beat. I won't be dancing just yet, but I have forgotten about the chances of meeting another bear as I take in my new surroundings.

I'm so glad to be on this adventure, playing in the forest. Perhaps I am finding a little rhythm as I bop and hop from stick to stone. I've not once tripped.

When I reach a clearing there is a choice of two paths to take. I'm not sure which way to go as Sally is the usual decision maker, but she's been quiet for a long time now, buried in my pocket.

'You can come out now, Sally.'

When she doesn't answer, I open my pocket to peer in on her. She is sitting with her wings behind her head, chomping on one of my sweets.

I'd forgotten I had them.

It's not the first sweet she's had - there are empty wrappers all around her. With her eyes closed, she is unaware I'm watching her. Without looking, she eats the last piece of a purple sweet from the wrapper in her hand.

It is funny to see the smile of delight on her face.

When she's ready for another one, she opens her eyes and forages amongst the empty wrappers. She has eaten nearly all of them.

'Erm, how about leaving one for me?' I ask.

Sally's head flicks round and her cheek feathers turn rosy red with embarrassment. She stops looking for another one and climbs out of my pocket before springing into action.

As she takes flight again, her belly bulges with all the sweets inside, and she hiccups. The force of it pushes her backwards and she flutters hard to propel herself forwards. It happens every time she hiccups and I can't help but laugh.

My tummy is tight with laughter as I watch the tears pour from her eyes as she giggles. Hiccups interrupt her then she giggles some more. She has to rest on my shoulder to stop laughing and wait for the hiccups to pass before she can catch her breath and take flight again.

'You are funny, Sally. I'm so glad you're here with me. Those sweets were a distant memory. I'd much rather watch you eat them when they're almost as big as you and make you ping around like a bursting balloon.'

I watch as she takes to the sky again, smiling and rubbing her belly as she looks around.

'Which way are we going?' she asks.

'I was hoping you would tell me. Which way is the water taxi?'

'Oh yes. Turn left,' she says, and I follow behind, stepping onto a new path to explore.

The path changes fast with every step and each bend brings a new shade of green. There are golden greens, vibrant greens, yellow greens and blue greens.

As we walk, the foliage begins to grow around us. It grows higher and higher until it forms a tunnel that arches over us. We are surrounded from the ground all the way over our heads.

We pass through in silence, watching everything that moves in this peaceful and enchanting place.

'Look at that butterfly, Sally. Her wings have colours like yours. But hers have holes in them. I wonder how she's able to fly?'

I step closer to examine its crumbling wings.

'It's amazing how beautiful she is, yet incomplete. Nature is amazing.'

When I turn away from the butterfly that seems like it might not last long, I notice a very shiny beetle to the right of Sally.

'Look at that,' I say, and point it out to Sally as she whizzes around to see it.

'It's ever so bright and shiny, just like my mother's silver earrings,' I say.

Then an elegant deer with an antlered head walks towards me. I stand still, hoping it doesn't run off. It holds my gaze, shifting its head from side-to-side, trying to work out what I am, I suppose. I smile hoping it will smile back, but it shakes its head instead and springs away from us.

It is out of sight quicker than it appeared.

I notice a family of rabbits playing together in the grass. Each one of them has different coloured fur with a tiny white cottontail bobbing along behind them. One is brown as chocolate, another is grey and white. There's a beige one, a black and white one with big floppy ears, and the smallest one of all is pure black. They're so cute and lovely, but I daren't try to pick one up as I'm not used to holding animals and these are wild rabbits. I don't know what they might do, and I don't want to scare them.

I leave them to busy on with their day.

When a funky smelling creature appears by my feet I'm not sure what to do. The smell gets worse when another one appears behind it. I watch as it rolls and frolics in the foliage. It seems intoxicated by the smell of the first one. I don't know why because it smells ever so stinky for something so dinky. I pinch my nose and pick up my pace to get out of their way.

As I run, I launch myself over a pile of raggedy red worms slithering over each other. They have big bulbous heads like boils. I'm not keen on them, but I don't want to squish them. I leap away, not paying attention to where I'm going and bash my head on a low branch of an old burnt out tree.

My head is sore so I give it a good rub to make it feel better, and find myself inches away from the long tongue of a light blue lizard. When it almost touches my lips, I step back to stay clear of a licking or a kissing.

I don't want its grimy germs on me.

As I turn to carry on, I crash into something that looks like a bench. Exhausted by all the walking, and the animals to avoid, I take a seat to rest my feet. But my weight is too much for the bench and it crashes to the floor, making a huge hole in the side of the tunnel. Before I can stop any more damage the tunnel crumbles. Snow pours in from the sky above, and before I know it, the entire canopy has collapsed.

Sally wasn't kidding about the cold snap. Heavy dumps of snow are now falling thick and fast. All the green has gone, and there is nothing but white around us.

Sally watches me zip up my coat, tie my scarf, and pull my hat over my ears.

'This is what I was afraid of,' she says.

'I've not seen anything like it,' I say. 'Look

at those trees. I can't believe my eyes.'

I stare in disbelief at the thick layer of snow covering the trees. It is so heavy they have curled into the shape of giant snails. I blink a few times to clear my eyes, as I can't decide if they're actually real snails. After all the other weird and wonderful things I've seen, there's no reason why they couldn't be. But one final blink confirms they are just trees.

I am grateful, as I don't know how I'd handle giant snails. Imagine all that slime.

We move on as the heavy snow continues to fall. Pretty snowflakes fall in clusters from the sky. They're much bigger than the ones I saw before. They settle on my arm and I'm able to inspect them.

'These snowflakes are wonderful, Sally. They sparkle and glitter, shine and shimmer, and they're much larger than I thought they could be.'

Before Sally can speak, her prediction of how unpredictable this forest can be soon rings true. The sky roars into a blizzard and fierce flows of snow drift towards us. It flows so thick that my feet are weighed down and I can't see ahead of me.

As the snow drags my feet, I find it difficult to walk. But Sally struggles more than I do as large clumps smack her tiny wings. Every dump knocks her sideways and the snow builds up on her wings. It weighs her down making it difficult to fly. She flutters hard to avoid dropping to the ground. I worry she won't be able to continue much longer.

I watch her for a while to make sure she's

okay, and when her eyelids droop for the fourth time, I pluck her from the sky. I rest her tired little body in the fold of my woolly warm scarf.

She'll be safe there.

'Thank you, Benjamin,' she mumbles.'

The snow is relentless as it continues to thicken. I start to struggle as it covers my feet, and I still can't see where I'm going. The light is dim and neither the sky nor sunshine lightens my way. Looking down, I can see no further than my thighs as my legs are buried in the snow from the knee down. It squeaks under my feet with every step I take, but I don't know what I'm walking towards.

I tread as lightly as I can, but catch my foot under something and fly forwards, landing face down in the snow. It provides a soft landing, but I struggle to clamber back to my feet. Every time I put a hand down to help push myself up, the snow moves and I have nothing to grasp.

'Are you okay, Benjamin?' asks a weak little Sally.

'Yes, but we must find shelter soon. I'll keep going for now. Rest up and stay warm in my scarf.'

I find it hard to go on, but I must keep trying. I take a deep breath to help calm me and focus my attention on the task. But there isn't a lot of air amongst the snow and I struggle to breathe. I pack the snow tight with my hands to give me something solid to push against, but disappear deeper and deeper into it with every attempt. It is tiring and I don't think I can find my way out.

Panic seeps though my heart as more and more snow piles in.

Then, as if my struggle is heard, it ends when the ground below me breaks away. I tumble down through the snow, falling and falling, to where, I don't know, but at least I can breathe.

I can't decide if I'm scared or relieved.

Chapter 14

Dropping faster and further than I have ever fallen before makes my stomach flip into frightened circles. My body spins and I have no idea which way is up or which way is down. I am once again feeling like I'm in the washing machine, but this time I am on a fast spin and it isn't very pleasant.

I brace myself for a hard landing, which comes with a thud as my rear bears the brunt and I am left dizzy and dazed. There will be a bruise on my bum tomorrow, but I'm glad, not glum, because I have stopped spinning and my quease has eased.

Now that I'm still, my eyes attempt to focus on the surrounding space. I am still and comfortable for the first time in what seems like forever.

I shift a little to assess my surroundings.

My nose awakens to smells around
as my ears listen and focus on sound.
Then my eyes clear to see a glow
of strange proportions that I don't know.

I'm on the floor under the ground
inside a home with people around.
Their pimpled faces look rather strange
as they stare from a table beside the range.

Their bodies are round with jelly in places
and bulges of green cover their faces.
But their eyes are soft and they don't look mean
so I smile back with a widening beam.

They wander over to take a peek
at this little person within their reach.
And despite their appearance, which plays on my
mind
they seem quite gentle and look rather kind.

'What's this?' beams a man with a strong
loud voice. He has a friendly but strange face and
his long finger is pointing right at me.

I half expect there to be a glob of snot on
the end of it like Caroline Clements' finger would,
but his finger is nice and clean. His voice sounds
like my great-grandfather who was Scottish.

He always brought us homemade gifts
when he came to visit. My favourite was a wooden
plaque that he'd inlaid with old coins. The idea
was to teach me what money looked like when he
was growing up.

I break my thoughts about my great-
grandfather when I realise I need to answer a
question.

'It's a scarf!' I say. It seems obvious, but I

don't know what this strange man knows of my world if he lives under the ground.

'No, ya silly boy, what do you have in yer scarf? It doesn't look very well.'

For a moment I have no idea what he's talking about. Then I remember that Sally is nestled in the fold of my scarf.

'Sally!' I gasp.

'What's a Sally?' asks a small girl in the corner of the room. She is climbing up the long skirt of a lady who might be her mother. The woman tries to prise open the girl's fingers, but she is a determined little thing. The woman picks her up instead.

'It's a bird, but its name is Sally. It... I mean she... is my friend. She wasn't feeling well, so I popped her in my scarf to keep her warm.'

The man steps closer, towering over me. 'Let me have that bird,' he says. His size intimidates me and my legs start to wobble. I put my hands up to protect myself from him.

'Go easy now, John,' says the lady of the house who is now heading my way with her little one held tight in her arms.

'No, you can't have her,' I shout. 'I have to take care of her. Please don't harm her.'

'Boy, you're in my home don't forget. Show a little trust for a fellow in his own home. She needs warming up. Hand her over before you lose her.'

'Don't worry little dear. My husband won't harm her. Hand her over to him and he'll make sure she's looked after,' says the woman before sitting back down at the table next to her little girl.

I'm embarrassed that I got it so wrong. I hand Sally over to him. She looks unwell with a strange blue-green tinge to her face. She looks so cold.

John surprises me by how tender he is with her. He wanders over to the fire and hovers her above the heat. I push all thoughts of him cooking her for dinner out of my head. I'm sure she'll be fine.

'This little lass is close to it,' says John. 'It's a good job you fell through the forest flap when you did. She's close to hyperthermia. I'll warm her up to get her blood flowing again. We'll know how she is with time. She's a special little thing, isn't she?'

'She sure is,' I answer, and then feel bad for thinking he might eat her.

'What were the two of you doing out there in this weather?' asks the lady. I watch as she piles a huge mound of wet food into the little girl's mouth until some of it trickles out.

'We're on our way to find a water taxi on the other side of the forest. We left home a long time ago, and it's time for us to return. Well it feels like we left a long time ago with all that has happened. The weather came in too quickly for us to find shelter and Sally's wings were growing too heavy for her to fly. I put her in my scarf to keep her warm then I fell through the forest floor.'

'It ain't called the Chillywhack Forest for nothing, son!' says John. 'But you did the right thing by burying the little treasure that she is in your scarf. She's far too little to handle those giant snowflakes. They can get as big as your head when the blizzards really kick in.'

My eyes widen with surprise. 'I understand that now, Sir. I might have lost her if I didn't hide her when I did.'

I watch John turn her over in his hand so she's now resting on her back. He spreads her wings wide so that all her feathers are separated and rubs her tiny tummy with his little finger.

'Is she going to be okay?' I ask.

'Yep, she'll be fine, Son. Her little heartbeat is growing stronger by the minute.'

Relief pours over me.

'I never expected that I would need to take care of her. She's always the strong one, but I wasn't sure if she'd survive the cold out there.'

'You did well, now go and sit with my wife Geraldine and get yourself something to eat.'

I look over to where she is sitting next to her little girl and she pats her hand on a seat, inviting me to sit next to her. My stomach rumbles and I remember that we haven't eaten for a long time.

The table is huge and close enough to the fire to leave a glow on their faces. They are surrounded by huge quantities of food in delightful colours. I want to leap in and try it all, but I wait until I'm invited.

'That's right dear, come over and help yourself. You must be ravenous by now.'

I don't know what that word means, but I am too hungry to ask. I am at the table and sitting down in a seat with a crispy golden chicken leg in my hand before I can blink. I am just about to put it in my mouth when Geraldine stops me by pushing my arm aside.

'Your wee little nose is running down your face. Let's wipe it up before your meal is disgraced.'

I'm embarrassed. But I suppose all my frozen bits are melting in the warmth of this room. It can't be helped.

When my face is clean, the lady waves her hand, encouraging me to eat. As I dive towards the chicken leg for the second time, I catch sight of the little girl staring at me.

'I'm sorry, is this your dinner I'm eating?'

'Oh don't you worry about that. There's plenty to go round. Little Daisy and I have more than we need and John was about to start his second helping when you crashed in.' Looking at his belly she adds, 'I don't think he needs a second helping, do you?' and she winks at her husband who is watching us from the other side of the room. 'You tuck in and enjoy your meal.'

With that I go full steam ahead, eating as much as I can stuff in. I eat so much that I forget to take a breath until I am so full I have to sit back in the chair. Releasing air from my tight lips, I look up for the first time and breathe.

Sally is standing in front of me with her arms folded. She taps the table with one of her funny bird feet, looking at me like she's waiting for me to say something.

'Is there anything left for me?' she asks with a smile on her face.

'I've made a special little plate for a special little girl,' says Geraldine.

Picking it up she places a meal of tiny multi-coloured beads in front of Sally. It isn't like anything I've seen before.

Sally munches away at the pretty beads, choosing a different colour each time she takes one. I don't know what they are, but she seems to like them as she sucks the juice from them and gulps them down as fast as she can.

She eats until her little feathered belly bulges so much that a feather pops out. 'Whoops!' exclaims Sally, and the whole room erupts with laughter. I laugh until my tummy aches.

After dinner, the family clear the table and move it away from the fire. They pull large leather chairs close to the heat and I am invited to take one for myself. My bottom is delighted to land on a mound of comfy cushions, as I sit myself down.

Sally flutters over to me and perches on my shoulder. It's all the space she needs to seat her tiny self.

John tells us lots of stories about other visitors they've had. It seems the snow has taken many people by surprise.

'What's the longest someone has stayed with you, John?' I ask.

'Now let me see. I'd say it was a good month that a little family stayed here last winter. They fell through the snow like you did. There were no tiny ones like Sally, but there were two children with their mother and father. I've not seen people look as cold as they did. The children's lips were icy blue and they shivered from their heads to their toes. They were so grateful to spend the time with us to wait for the terrible weather to pass.'

'I think they stayed more than a month,' says Geraldine. 'I remember the snow had cleared but the children needed more time to grow their strength before they could get going again. We fed and fattened those little loves until they were round enough to roll out of here and bounce along smiling again.'

Geraldine chuckles with delight at the memory, as she stirs a saucepan of milk over the fire. I watch her sieve chocolate powder into the milk and add a big spoon of something that looks like lumpy honey. It reminds me of the last time my mother made me a hot chocolate. I was little.

This is the first time I've thought about her since I left home. I wonder if she's still asleep? If she's awake she'll be wondering where I am and will soon blame Dad for my disappearance.

When Geraldine finishes making the hot chocolate, she passes a mug to each one of us, except Sally. Her hands are too small to hold one. She gets a tiny thimble turned upside down instead. She steadies it for Geraldine to pour the last of the liquid into it.

I blow cool air onto mine until I think it has reached the right temperature for me. I sip and suck air in at the same time to stop it from burning my mouth. The temperature is perfect and it is the most delicious thing I have ever tasted.

It is bliss in a mug.

'What can I taste, Geraldine? Is it honey?'

'Oh no, I don't use honey. You can taste my special homemade marmalade. It's sweeter than any marmalade you might have had before. I use local oranges that grow in the warmth of the summer. They're rare and the tastiest you'll find.

The farmers don't spray the oranges with mucky pesticides on this land. I watch the oranges grow until they're perfect for picking. You won't find better marmalade anywhere.'

Sally smacks her lips together as she slurps hers down.

'Did you like that?' I ask.

'Yes, sir,' she says, as she wipes the back of her hand across her face to clear the excess milk away.

When we tire, Geraldine shows us to a room with two fluffy beds she's made up for us. My bed is in a bathtub filled with a duvet and pillows, and Sally's is in the sink with the same bedding as mine. I watch as Daisy tucks in Sally, and then Geraldine throws more bedding over each of us. We are soon cosy and ready to sleep.

'Good night children and sleep well.'

I'm asleep before I can reply with thanks,
but I am oh so grateful.

Chapter 15

Waking to the most beautiful shimmery sunshine filtering through the window is a treat after the previous day's cold. I am surprised to see the sky though, as I thought we were under the ground.

Never mind, I lay still for a little while, enjoying the warmth on my skin, cosy under my fluffy duvet. I'd like to stay here all day, but it's time for us to move on. The family have been so good to us. We mustn't overstay our welcome.

'Sally, are you ready to go? We should let these kind people get on with their day.

'I was thinking the same thing just this very second, Benjamin.'

We peel back our covers, shake ourselves free, and step out of our makeshift beds. Then Geraldine comes through the door, her arms filled with goods.

'Good morning my little ones, you're both looking much rosier today. You'll be pleased to know that all the snow has cleared and the house is no longer buried. It's a bright and wonderful day.'

'Are you saying that the house isn't underground?' I ask.

'Oh no, my little cherub, we're certainly

not under the ground. That was a heavy snowfall yesterday. We were snowed in. It's a miracle you fell through it. Can I get you some breakfast?'

'Thank you, but we should leave soon to make the most of the daylight to help us on our way.'

'I thought you might say that, and it's a wise thing to do. I've packed a knapsack with food for you to take on your journey.'

'That's very kind of you, Geraldine.'

'Oh not at all. Now just so you know...

The land is dry
No snowflakes in site
But it changes fast with cold full of might.

I've packed you a blanket and a set of skis -
If it comes in fast you must ski free.'

She wags her finger at us to exaggerate her words, but we understand all too well.

'You must move faster than it follows, you understand?'

I nod and take the knapsack that holds a blanket and food. There are skis crossed on the back. I have no idea how to use them, but I'm sure Sally can help me.

The three of us head in to the living room to join John and Daisy. They have gathered to say goodbye and are standing in the same spot I landed on yesterday.

'Thank you for the food and the fun - we'll

never forget you for taking us in, and for saving Sally,' I say.

'Not a problem, boy,' says John.

Sally beams at him with more thanks than her words can say, but we all know how grateful she is.

'Now the two of you must take care out there. It shouldn't take too long for you to get to the water taxi, but you must keep moving. Don't stop for anything, especially bears. They're stirring in the forest this time of year.'

'Yes they are. We already tried to wake one yesterday and regretted it,' says Sally

'Why on earth would you play a game like that?' asks John. 'No, don't answer that, just don't do it again. They're not to be meddled with when they're sleepy and hungry. Nobody needs a grouchy bear on their hands.'

Sally and I give each other a knowing smile as we wave to the family over our shoulders.

We leave the house through the front door, shouting our goodbyes to John, Geraldine, and Daisy before wandering back into the forest. There isn't a snowflake in site as the sunshine twinkles a comforting haze through the trees.

It's a beautiful day.

Chapter 16

'Weren't they the nicest people you've ever met, Sally?'

'They were, and we reached them just in time,' she says, and hovers close to my shoulder. It reminds me of how I nearly lost her the last time she did that.

'I feared losing you to the cold, and I didn't know what to do to help you. Thank goodness for that wonderful family.'

'Yes, they were marvellous, but you helped me more than you realise. I felt so warm and safe in your scarf. I am so grateful to you.'

'That's what good friends are for, isn't it? You would do the same for me,' and I smile at her, thrilled to have her by my side.

'Of course I would. But still, you acted like an expert and I'm grateful.'

An expert? Maybe I am a real adventurer now. My feet certainly feel lighter and surer of themselves now that the snow has gone.

Sally and I travel along in the quiet of the forest and take in our new surroundings. But after a while of walking, I feel uneasy about the direction we're going.

'Sally, I'm not so sure we'll find water in this part of the forest.'

'What makes you say that?' she asks.

'Well, the trees are thinning the further we walk and although the snow has gone so has the lush green of the forest we saw before. Doesn't that suggest there's no water around here?'

'Come on, Benjamin; don't be a pessimist. Nothing else has been what we first thought on this trip. I think we're getting close to where the river should be. Let's just keep going.'

I grunt, not feeling optimistic. When we step out of the trees into a clearing where the ground is barren I see no trace of water.

As if Sally can read my mind, she asks, 'have you ever thought about the possibility of your needs and desires being the things that create your opportunities?'

This seems like another of her mind-bending conversations that I get lost with, but I think I know where she's going with it.

'I can't just make things appear, Sally. I'm not a magician.'

'Who said you couldn't? We want a water taxi, don't we?'

This confirms she's off on a tangent that I'm probably not going to understand, but I go along with it to see where it leads.

'Yes we do want a water taxi, Sally.'

'And for that we need water.' She stares at me waiting for agreement. 'Am I right?' she asks, forcing a response from me.

116

'Yes.'

'Well it's that simple, Benjamin.'

'Oh now you're just being silly. I'm not interested in going back through all that nonsense. It confuses me. Besides, look where we are. There is nothing here. It's too dry even for trees. Logic rules over any kind of magic.'

'Silly, am I?'

Sally flies on ahead looking unhappy and I struggle to keep up with her.

'Well, you're not silly, but just because I want something, it doesn't mean I can always have it,' but she's not listening. She's too busy humming to herself as she flutters on ahead.

I think about being able to see things in different ways as I try to catch up with her. But I'm not sure how that extends to creating things from scratch.

I've never been good at getting my own way with requests at home, no matter how hard I've tried.

When I get closer to Sally I try to ask her a question, but her humming turns into a rant.

'Snip-snap-splat -
what shall I do
to make you see what's in front of you?

Patience: that's all you need
to flee from the desert and the trees.

117

The river will swell and surge through the ground
filling this well with water abound.

For life to go on in all of its beauty -
just open your eyes and don't get snooty.

The more you believe the quicker it comes
to show you how life lives by the drum.'

Sally sounds impatient with me and I'm not sure what to say. Her words do make sense, and she's sounding more and more like Willow every day.

I suppose I should have faith if I want to keep my adventurous spirit. The idea of going on an adventure seemed impossible a few days ago, yet here I am.

I don't want it to be my last adventure.

Before I can apologise to Sally, I hear her screaming.

I turn to ask her what's wrong.

'Quick, lift your feet and get ready to paddle, a swell is coming and you won't be able to wade out of this one,' she shouts.

She's right.

I spot a huge gush of water far in the distance, rolling fast down the mountains.

I can't tell how far I need to go to be safe, but I must move fast because I won't be able to paddle through it when it comes.

I run after Sally, trusting her sense of

direction. But as I run I realise we're in a riverbed and it's the only place the water will want to go.

Chapter 17

Bursting through the trees, a huge torrent of water pours its way into the dry riverbed. I think about Sally's words. I do want a water taxi, which requires water to float, and here I am running from all the water I need to help me get home, but if I don't move fast enough I'll drown.

It's a confusing conflict.

'Run faster, Benjamin! If you don't move now, you'll be washed away before you know what to do with yourself.'

I leap as high and as far as I can, landing face down on a mound of soil that goes up my nose. Air heaves out of my lungs as I look up to check where I am.

I am safe on the riverbank with only one foot left dangling over the edge. Then a huge wave surges in and rolls over my foot. I lose my shoe with the rage of the current.

Too exhausted to move, I lay on the riverbank, feeling nothing but my sock being tugged from my foot. I look behind to find a huge salmon sucking on it and kick it off to stop it tickling my toes. The salmon flies into the air and lands with a splash.

'What is it with waves, Sally? That's the second one I've avoided now.'

I think over that point for a while as I roll over to relax my bones in the heat of the sun.

The things that have happened to me since I left home have been incredible.

My thirst for adventure is quenched.

As I look around, I feel I'm exactly where I should be, out in the great outdoors with my best friend by my side.

'Happy, are we?' asks Sally, as she rolls her eyes and giggles at me.

'Yes I am as a matter of fact,' and I blow a raspberry, knowing it will annoy her. I smile because I know she's pretending to ignore me, but at least she doesn't look angry anymore.

'Glad to hear it, but perhaps you should wander over here towards me. You'll be wiped out in seconds if you stay there and another wave comes along. There's no Willow to save you now.'

'Willow! The day, day and night, the week or weeks... how long has it been since I spoke to Willow? It seems like a lifetime ago.'

'But it isn't, and you've already forgotten the lesson he taught you. Now will you get over here?'

I move towards Sally and absorb how the once dried out valley is now breathing with life. It is a magical place, filled with birds and butterflies fluttering around. Salmon jump with the watery spray, sucking at the air above them before splashing back down.

They remind me of a television programme I once saw. The river was filled with so much salmon that bears came from everywhere to catch them for their dinner.

Bears!

I feel a little wobbly at the thought of them, just as I spot three of them across the water. There are two big ones and a baby. But I feel safe, as the river grows wider between them and us with every raging rapid that pours down the valley.

I watch as the big bear kisses the little one on the nose. They can be so nice to each other.

Maybe they're only grumpy and grizzly when they first wake up. I feel like that myself when it's pouring down with rain and I have to go to school.

I take a deep breath and wander back towards the water. Sally hovers by my side and I splash her when she least expects it. She tries not to laugh, but I know that she likes it, even if her arms are folded.

I laugh anyway.

When the unexpected sound of a car horn interrupts me, I turn around to find a man in what looks like a little boat on the water. Or is it a car?

It's yellow with lights and has doors like a car. But if it's on the water it can't have wheels. They don't work on water.

'Hey mate, you need a taxi?'

'Sally, a water taxi!'

I am overjoyed. With a water taxi we can go home. It's been a fun adventure, but it's also been tough for my first one and I'm tired.

I look at the water taxi and finally understand what one is because it looks like a boat and a car rolled into one.

'Oi mate, I ain't no Sally, and I ain't got all day. I can catch another fare up the bank. Now shake a leg if you wanna hop on.'

Rather than shaking a leg, I skip into a run to get to the taxi as quickly as I can. I want to make sure nobody gets it before we do.

Not that we've seen anyone for a while, but you never know.

'So where are we going, mate?' asks the driver.

'Sally?' I turn towards her, but she's gone.

'I have wings, darling; I'm on the roof.'

Leaning out of the taxi, I pull myself up to peer over the roof to where Sally is sitting. She is glistening in the sunlight. Her wings are behind her head, her arms and legs crossed, her eyes are closed, and her big smile fills her face.

'Go with the wind, Benjamin,' she says without opening her eyes.

'Look, mate, yer on a meter, either we get moving or you get out. There's always another punter to pick up.'

'Home please. She knows they way,' I say, pointing towards the roof. I don't want to waste an opportunity to catch a taxi home. It's been a long old journey for my first adventure.

'Alright,' says the driver, 'but you're in for a ride if she's your navigator.'

As purple glitter falls around me I suspect it's from Sally. It swirls around my seatbelt and buckles me in. I feel safe and secure just in time for the taxi to speed away. It accelerates fast enough to slam me hard into my seat.

The taxi skims along a tight bend in the river then slides sideways to avoid rocks before shooting forwards into fierce rapids that bounce us around. When the water flattens out again, the vehicle glides for a while and I relax. But it's not long before we hit more crazy rapids then slow once again.

This is a crazy ride.

When it calms I take the opportunity to peer out of the open window for the first time.

I can't believe my eyes.

'Sally, I know you have wings, but we've just taken off higher than I think you've flown before.'

The water taxi is soaring over a waterfall. We've reached a scary height and I feel queasy with fear. I'm petrified of us falling and crashing to the ground. But my fears are unnecessary as two huge bronze wings sprout from the sides of the taxi - we're flying

Lifting high above the water, we avoid the trees and the mountains ahead as we swoop up in a big arc towards the clouds.

'Wow, Sally, this is crazy. Look at all that snow down there - it's beautiful.'

'It is, and to think we were amongst it not so long ago.' She smiles but her body shudders and

I imagine she is thinking back to when the cold got to her.

Sally snaps back to the present in an instant.

'Don't get too comfortable, Benjamin; this is a water taxi after all. It prefers water to flight.'

Chapter 18

Diving faster and faster until it hits the water the water taxi plunges deep. Water fills my nose until I can't breathe and the last air bubble leaves me.

Then, just as I gasp for breath, my seat belt releases and I burst free through the open window. I try to swim to the surface and expect to bob to the top and float down a stream.

But the water pours me through a hole in a jagged brick wall.

Landing with a thud in a dark damp place, I am a little shaken, but certainly not stirred, as I wonder where I am.

The water, Sally and the water taxi have all disappeared.

Sitting in the dark, I don't understand what has happened. But I'm not scared, just lightheaded after all the flying around. I wonder if I'm amongst the glittery dust of Willow again, but my nose isn't tickling.

I rub my eyes hoping to see
what there could be in front of me.

All is clear at the end of my nose
so I search on ahead in sopping wet clothes.

I squelch along weary and scared
but braver this time I move undeterred.

I've seen so much in such a short time
that I know I'll be fine if I just keep a line.

So step-by-step I slowly go -
where in the end
I really don't know.

But sure in my step and as brave as I can
I keep on walking like a full-grown man.

At the end of the way in the cave that I entered
I find a door right in the centre.

It's a little door of familiar frame -
I want to knock, but is it a game?

I feel around from the top to the ground
when the tiny door pops from its frame.

Careful in step I slowly move
from the dark of a cave to a familiar place.

I find myself remarkably safe
in the midst of my room with my bed unmade.

Tired and worn I lead with my head
all the way to my little warm bed.

My weary eyes close down gently
so I lay down cosy and heavy as lead.

Chapter 19

Stirring from a deep sleep I feel the back of a hand touching my forehead. It's Mum. She is smiling down on me when my eyes open.

'There you are. We were worried about you last night. You were thrashing around and talking nonsense in your sleep. You had such a high fever. We nearly took you to the hospital.'

It must have been a dream and I feel sad.

'If it wasn't for your lovely friend, Sally, you might have found yourself in trouble out in that awful weather yesterday. She found you down by the water all sodden and shivery. She ran up to the house to ask your father to collect you. He had to pick you up and carry you home.'

This is all a big surprise. It means I made it down to the shoreline, but suggests that Willow didn't save me from a huge incoming wave.

'Are you saying that Sally saved me down at the bottom of the road, Mum?'

'Yes, she did. You can thank her later, but for now, get yourself a little more rest. I'll come and check on you in a few hours.'

I can't believe what has happened. How can we not have gone on a real adventure? I'll be so disappointed. But I'm not about to believe it until I can investigate a few things.

When Mum leaves the room, I listen to make sure she has made it all the way down the stairs before I throw back my covers. Then I creep out of bed to avoid her hearing me and tiptoe over to the little door to the eaves cupboard without making a sound.

I open the door only wide enough to squeeze my body through. I don't like it in here because it's cold. The only light comes from my bedroom, shining through the door, and as I walk the length of the house it gets darker the further I walk from it.

But I focus my mind on my mission as I felt safe enough in here earlier and it's the same space. I've just got to find the hole at the end.

As I walk along the length of the house it's not as dark as I expected. I trail a finger along the wall to help keep me balanced as I tiptoe along.

But when I reach the end, I let out the loudest cry, forgetting my need to be silent. There isn't a cave or a hole in the wall and the ground is dry. There is no way I could have poured in here with water from the river.

I am sad as I examine the dry ground and realise it was all just a dream.

I turn back with my head hung low. If there isn't a cave and no water around then none of it was real. I return to my room, back through the little door I thought I entered hours before. Closing it behind me, as I thought I had before, I jump back into bed and drift off to sleep feeling disappointed.

Chapter 20

Waking again, at whatever o'clock it might be, I have no idea what day it is. I go downstairs to find my parents sitting in their usual spots in front of the television. But this time they're sitting closer together and Mum seems happier. Before I can join them there is a knock at the door and I walk over to answer it.

As so few people come to the house, I am always intrigued to find out who it might be.

My excitement doubles when I open the door to find Sally standing there. Correction, my excitement quadruples, as she'll be able to answer my questions.

She'll know whether I've been ill and asleep or outside bouncing around to the beat of my drum.

Then I remember that she isn't supposed to come here anymore. I look across to my parents who are both smiling. It must be okay. These telepathic conversations are becoming more and more frequent in my life.

I think I'm learning to understand them.

Sally and I chat in the doorway about how well I am, but all I want to talk about is our adventure. The problem is that my parents are in earshot and they clearly don't know about it. They think I've been in bed sick all day, but I hope I'm just tired from all of our travels.

We talk about school and Josephine. It goes on for longer than I'd like and I'm not paying attention as my mind wanders off.

I need to know if we went an adventure.

My chance comes when she says she has to go home and steps away from the front door.

Before she leaves the porch, I lean out and whisper to her.

'Sally, we went on an adventure yesterday, didn't we?'

'I don't know what you're talking about, Benjamin Frank.'

I'm startled by her response and disappointment floods my veins. But as she steps off the porch, she turns to look at me over her shoulder. Tiny bits of purple glitter sprinkle from her eyelashes as she winks at me and her cheeks burn a rosy shade of red. Then she wanders off.

The wink and the glitter tell me we must have been on an adventure. But how can I know for sure?

I shut the door behind me, feeling flummoxed. But when I look down, my spirits lift as I spot a tiny, peacock green feather lying on the floor. As it shimmers with purple glittery radiance, it is all I need to confirm that we went on an adventure.

The biggest smile spreads across my face

and I decide that from now on, my life will be nothing but the adventure I make it. I am so happy after everything that has happened.

Excitement fills me from the top of my head to the tip of my toes.

I pass my parents at full speed as I run off to plan my next adventure. I know what to do next time, and I can do it all by myself. But I also know that I'll have more fun if Sally comes along.

I might wait until the summer though, as I've had enough of bears and changeable weather for a while, even though I now know how to handle them.

Before I leave the living room, Dad calls out to me and switches off the television. My body begins to boil as I suspect I'm in trouble.

'Benjamin, we're sorry if things have been difficult around here for a while. We're also sorry you felt you had to run away.'

I am amazed that my father has noticed my feelings. It makes me smile to know he cares.

'That's okay, Dad.'

'We also realise that we've not shown you all the things out there that are important for you to see,' says Mum.

What on earth has got in to my parents since I've been away? I must have been away for longer than they realise.

'How about we all go out together next weekend? We can show you around,' says Dad and Mum turns to him and smiles.

'Yes please. I'd like that Dad.'

'That's settled then. I won't work next weekend and we'll all go out together.'

I run off to my room before they change their minds, my belly filled with puzzled delight.

What just happened?

When I reach the top of the stairs, I remember something very important and run back down to ask my parents.

'Can Sally come over again?'

'Yes,' says Mum. 'We're sorry about all that. She's always welcome here.'

I am up the stairs again in seconds. The adults have sorted out whatever their problem was and are friends again. What a difference a day or two makes. Or was it a week? I'm sure I'll work it out when I go back to school. Oh no - school!

I begin to hope for another tremendous tide to come along and wash me away. It might save me from having to sit with Stella and the rest of the crazy crew.

But if my adventure has taught me anything, it has taught me how to handle difficult situations. I am now more than capable of handling them even if I have a little wobble once in a while.

Jungle James is nothing compared to the might of a grizzly bear or a tremendous tide.

THE END

Benjamin's Journey

A tremendous tide pours into town
revealing a bird wearing a crown.

Then a whirly willow saves the day
from crazy waves that clear the bay.

A timely tune sings along
through strange encounters all day long.

As simple sight brings dreams alive
for new ideas to be applied.

On a joyous journey that opens the heart
to new beginnings right from the start.

A Grizzly Bear might cloud the day
but plans are hatched to run away.

As forest friends will come along
to pave the way and sing a song.

Side by side
Arm in arm
Giving thanks
Free from harm.

As fleeing free is so much fun
when sharing life out in the sun.

So get out there and find your spirit
life is short - make sure you live it.

Acknowledgements

I'd like to thank my friends and family for their patience in giving me the space and time I've needed to write The Adventures of Benjamin Frank. It's been fantastic fun to write, but it's a struggle to find the energy on top of a demanding day in the office.

Thank you to my editor, Sally Munson. We met at work and her inability to accept poor grammar was exactly what I needed to make sure this book made it through quality control. She has been supportive and kind with her recommendations.

To everyone good enough to read various drafts, thank you for your time, encouragement and feedback. It takes effort to get the right story written. You've all helped me to manage that process and stay true to the story. Special thanks to Natalie Miles and Khurrum Rahman for their constructive input.

Thank you to my brother, David Skilling and my buddy Ashimi Adefesobi for their input with the cover design. I went from doodling to deciding to do the cover myself. Their guidance helped me to reach my vision.

It takes courage to do something out of the ordinary and sometimes it's when courage wavers that you wonder why you're spending so much time on something that might not be worth pursuing. Your heart knows to continue but your mind sometimes tells another story. That story can be damaging and potentially stop you from following through. Thank you to all who have supported me to ignore my doubts and continue the positive act of writing this story. It's a journey and I'm fortunate to have fantastic people travel along with me.

I have some incredible people in my life with the ability to reflect my light back at me even when I can't see it myself. It keeps me strong, maintains my momentum and refills me with faith to keep me going. The little reminders and affirmations mean a lot, either through words or a much needed hug.

Thank you.

Made in the USA
Charleston, SC
18 November 2015